A NOVEL BY
MARK MOORER

© 2026 Mark Moorer

Illustrations by Mark Moorer

All rights reserved.

No part of this book may be reproduced or transmitted in any form or by any means, including graphics, electronic, or mechanical, including photocopying, recording, taping, or by any information storage or retrieval system, without the permission in writing from the author and publisher.

Published by Little Studio Films

ISBN: 979-8-9930592-9-7
LCCN: 2026904189

Edited by: Fernanda Oetling
Cover by: Mark Moorer

For my wife, Riley, Jace, Alec, Trey, MeMe, and Gampy.

Author's Note

Growing up on the Gulf Coast, I was surrounded by the lore and legends of pirates. Tales of salt-stained seas and daring adventures fired my imagination from a young age. Every other summer, my grandparents would take us to Disney World. A trip I always counted down to with excitement.

 My grandfather's favorite ride was Pirates of the Caribbean. It became mine as well. After our family had all ridden the iconic attraction, my grandfather, J.R. Hall, whom us grandkids lovingly called "Gampy"—and I would linger behind to ride it again. He'd lean in close and say, in his gravelly voice, "Let's go again." I loved it. And the ride attendants were never going to say no to an eighty-year-old man and his ten-year-old grandson. Together, Gampy and I would ride at least two more times before the rest of the family returned to collect us. Because of those moments—because of him—I dedicate this book to my grandfather, J.R. Hall, "Gampy." And when I look toward heaven now, I smile and whisper, "Let's go again, Gampy. Let's go again."

Contents

The Tale Begins

The Caribbean 1725. The sun bleeds into the sea, painting the sky in bruised purples and angry oranges. A spectacle mirrored in the turbulent waves that crash against the jagged black volcanic rocks lining the secluded cove. Palm trees, their fronds whipping in the restless sea breeze, wave at the bruised twilight sky. Their shadows were long and distorted by the firelight. Along the serene shoreline, a bonfire crackles, a malevolent heart beating at the center of a ring of men. Their faces flickered in the hellish light, revealing the grime ingrained in their skin. Exhaustion etched into their features, years of battling unforgiving life at sea. The sand, coarse and black like ground charcoal, crunches underfoot, hot even as the sun dips below the horizon. Salt spray stings the nostrils, mingling with the acrid scent of wood smoke, the pungent aroma of roasting meat, and something else... something metallic, coppery, clinging to the humid air; the metallic tang is almost unbearably sharp.

Benjamin Hornigold, a mountain of a man whose shadow alone seems to consume the meager expanse of sand, stokes the flames with his sword, a wickedly curved blade that gleams like a predator's tooth, its polished surface reflecting the fiery embers. In the distance, a clipper ship, its skeletal shape casting watery reflections against the dying light, sat anchored in the cove. Its tattered sails hang limp, a silent and ominous witness to the dark story unfolding. The rhythmic creak of its timbers underscores the uneasy silence between the men, broken only by the crackle of the fire and the rhythmic lap of the waves. A single, watchful frigate bird circles overhead, a dark silhouette against the fiery sky, its piercing cry swallowed by the vastness of the ocean.

Hornigold's voice, a gravelly rasp honed by rum and years of violence, cuts through the night. "I knew a man," he rasped, his eyes burning with a glow that rivaled the bonfire, "a man who rewrote the rules of the world. Everyone whispered his name, a prayer or a curse, depending on who you asked. But I knew him before the whispers began, before the legend was born. Before he even had a name." He pauses, a shudder passing through his powerful frame; the memory washes over him like falling rain. "It was a time... a moment... so fleeting, so incandescently brief, that the edges blur. The details... they slip like sand through my fingers, leaving only a ghost of what was. Some details slip through my memory. But

I can tell you how the feeling of it still claws at my soul..." His gaze drifts to the restless ocean, and a distant memory emerges, mirroring the gathering darkness.

A maelstrom of splintered timbers and churning, blood-flecked water. Three ships, locked in a brutal, desperate ballet of death off the smoking slopes of St. Vincent. The air, thick with the stench of salt spray, burning powder, and the coppery tang of spilled blood, clawed at their lungs. The Robert and The Avenger, their black flags obscene, mocking parodies of surrender, flapped like the wings of carrion birds, their prey cornered.

The Caribbean in 1717 was a wild place. A festering wound, a crucible forged in greed and drowned in blood. Pirates were devils in that emerald hell, their souls already forfeit. The prize that day was the Concord, a French galleon, swollen with the ill-gotten riches of empires. A magnificent beast, yes, but her beauty was a mask for the suffering within. That day... that day, paradise choked on the screams of the dying.

Chaos reigned. Not merely a symphony of screams, but a cacophony of agony, the splintering of bone echoing the crack of shattering timber, the guttural roar of cannon fire a death knell for hope. Smoke, thick and acrid as the densest soot, choked the air, clinging to the blood-slicked planks like a shroud. Through the hellish haze, two figures emerged, their presence a physical blow, silencing the panic like a sudden, suffocating pressure. Edward Teach, a colossus of a man, his coarse black hair a tangled nest of vipers, his braided beard a writhing serpent reaching his chest, each strand thick with the grease of the spoils of war. And Hornigold, beside him, his eyes glittering with predatory intelligence that chilled the very marrow.

Their approach alone stilled the frantic scrambling, a palpable tension freezing terror into the very souls of the men. They moved like wraiths of vengeance, their aura of violence a tangible force, a suffocating wave of absolute dominance crushing the Frenchmen's resistance. They reached the French captain, a broken puppet held aloft by Teach's brutal crew, his eyes mirroring the terror that gnawed at his heart. A testament to their merciless power. A silence, thick and suffocating, heavy with the scent of fear, spilled rum, and the coppery tang of death, descended. Then Hornigold's voice, when it cut through the stillness, was a blade honed to razor sharpness, a whisper that promised exquisite, agonizing torment.

The salt spray stung Hornigold's face, the reek of brine burning canvas and blood thick in the air. His eyes, cold chips of flint, fixed on the Frenchman.

"Speak English, you sniveling cur," he rasped, the words a whip cracking in the wind. A guttural chuckle rumbled from the pirates, a chorus of anticipation that scraped against D'Ocier's soul. Captain D'Ocier, his face ashen, stammered a weak "Yes."

Hornigold's smile was a predatory gleam. "Three questions. Answer wrongly, and the sea will be your grave."

The laughter intensified, a wave of predatory glee crashing over the deck. The rhythmic creak of the ship, the harsh cry of gulls overhead, all muted by the rising dread.

"Your name? Your destination? Your cargo?" Hornigold's gaze, briefly meeting Teach's, a shared understanding passing between two titans of brutality, hardened again. He felt the French captain's terror like a physical thing.

D'Ocier began, his voice a thread of fear, "My name is Jean D'Ocier..." But the words died in his throat. Hornigold's hand, a vise of iron, clamped over his mouth, silencing the confession before it was complete.

"I know your cargo," Hornigold snarled, a cruel twist to his lips. He gestured to Teach, a silent handover of this human plaything.

Teach, a whirlwind of dark energy, stepped forward. His eyes, twin pools of molten obsidian, bored into D'Ocier's soul. The air crackled with the unspoken promise of violence. He moved with a grace that belied the brutal intent, a panther toying with its prey. "What shall we do with him?" The question hung in the air, a venomous invitation.

The pirates 'cries were a cacophony of bloodlust. "Run him through!" "Feed him to the sharks!" The words were punctuated by the rasp of steel on steel as Teach drew his cutlass and his sword, twin daggers of death gleaming in the harsh light. With terrifying swiftness, he plunged both weapons into the captain's gut.

The roar of the sea swallowed D'Ocier's gasp, a choked sob,. His eyes, wide with unimaginable horror, met Teach's before the light fled them. The pirates, two hulking brutes, heaved D'Ocier's corpse overboard. It struck the water with a sickening thud, a final, silent scream lost in the waves.

One by one, the sailors threw the bound Frenchmen, screaming curses in their native tongue, into the churning sea. The soldiers showed no mercy and cut down the few who tried to fight. The triumphant yells of the pirates swallowed the shrieks and splashes.

The deck ran red.

Teach, his face smeared with blood, raised his sword. A triumphant, chilling laugh tore from his chest, a sound born of power and carnage. "Did I miss anyone's pleasure?" The crew roared their approval, a symphony of savagery echoing across the blood-soaked deck. Hornigold, a grim smile playing on his lips, watched from the stern, the master puppeteer of this terrifying spectacle. The scent of salt, blood, and victory hung heavy in the air, a testament to their brutal dominance.

The Pirate Republic

Blackbeard, along with eight men, accompanied Hornigold in a longboat to the shores of New Providence. Pirates lined the shoreline, their faces grim and expectant. A suffocating silence clung to the small craft, broken only by the rhythmic slap of oars. As the longboat grated on the sand, two pirates waded out to assist. Hornigold disembarked, his usual swagger a little less pronounced. Blackbeard followed, his gait heavier than usual, each step a deliberate effort against the churning in his gut.

Hornigold's crew unloaded their captain's belongings, a pathetically small pile compared to the treasures Blackbeard had seen him amass. James Blair, a skinny, weathered man with long strands of grey hair, stepped forward. "It's been a long time, mate!"

"Aye." Hornigold's voice was flat, lacking its usual boisterous cheer.

“Will you be staying long?” Blair extended his hand to Hornigold. It was a handshake that conveyed a silent greeting understood by only certain pirates.

"Consider me at home," Hornigold replied, but the words sounded hollow, even to his own ears. The mutual understanding between the two men felt brittle, fragile. Hornigold patted Blair on the shoulder, a gesture that felt both perfunctory and heavy with unspoken things, then turned to Blackbeard.

This moment, this quiet farewell, was a luxury most pirates never afforded. Blackbeard knew it, a bitter twist of recognition tightening in his chest. He saw it as a betrayal of everything they had both fought for, a surrender to the insidious comfort of a settled life, a life Blackbeard had sworn he'd never have.

The thought pricked at his conscience, a voice whispering of the life he could have had, a life he'd ruthlessly abandoned. He gave Hornigold one last nod, a gesture stiff with unspoken resentment, the weight of a broken promise.

"If you need anything... sanctuary, port, or if you just want the pleasure of my company... you know where I am."

"Aye," Blackbeard managed, his beard curling into a grim imitation of a grin. The words felt like a lie, a hollow offering from a man already plotting his escape from this stifling sense of obligation. He couldn't bear the thought of his mentor, his teacher, his *friend* living this quiet, almost respectable existence, abandoning the life they'd shared. The envy burned like acid.

Blackbeard's men began boarding the longboat. He tipped his hat at Hornigold, the gesture perfunctory, devoid of warmth.

"Captain."

"Captain."

With a swift, almost frantic turn, Blackbeard hopped into the boat. Two men shoved them off. He sat with his back to the shoreline, the silence on the return to the Concord deafening. The weight of his unspoken accusations, his unspoken envy, and his unspoken longing for a life he knew he could never have pressed down on him. He had chosen violence and ruthlessness, but the quiet, agonizing regret was far more painful. He had chosen to abandon Hornigold to a life he secretly craved, a life he knew he could never reach. And that, he knew, was a choice he would regret for the rest of his violent, short life.

Hornigold looks out toward The Concord and The Avenger. The long boat has nearly reached its destination. A knot of unease tightens in his gut. "Bring hell with you," he mutters, the words tasting like ash in his mouth. This new chapter was his choice. He gave Blackbeard everything, seduced by the promise of untold riches, but the recklessness of

it, the sheer brutality, now gnaws at his conscience.
He'd always prided himself on a certain…honor
among thieves. This? This was something else
entirely.

Blackbeard boards the Concord as his men secure
the longboat. The air crackles with a feverish energy,
a brutal efficiency that chills Hornigold to the bone.
Men swarm the deck like angry hornets. Blackbeard,
a whirlwind of black hair and shadowed eyes,
ascends the small flight of stairs at the stern. He
turns, his gaze sweeping over the crew, a predator
assessing its prey. Hornigold sees a flicker of
something… doubt? … in Blackbeard's eyes, but it's
gone in an instant, replaced by the familiar mask of
ruthless ambition.

"Weigh anchor!" Blackbeard roared, his voice a
thunderclap. "Rouse the watch forward! It's time we
be on our way!"

The men sprang into action, a chaotic ballet of
violence and efficiency. Hornigold watches, his
stomach churning. He'd envisioned sharing the
spoils, living a life of comfortable excess. But the
cost… the blood… it's a price he's starting to
question if he can truly afford. He sees a young sailor,
barely a man, stumble as he tries to hoist a sail, his
face pale with fear. Hornigold wants to intervene, to
ease the suffering, but the weight of his own

complicity pins him to the spot. He's already crossed a line; there's no turning back. To leave now would be cowardly, foolish...and likely fatal. But to stay...to continue down this path of bloodshed...that's a fate he increasingly dreads. He clenches his fists; the choice to stay and embrace his new home, or to abandon his newfound allies and face certain death– a bitter pill he's forced to swallow. The Robert remained behind at the port of New Providence, a silent witness to his last ride. He knows, with a sickening certainty, that he will regret this day.

The harsh Caribbean sun stung Hornigold's face as he and Blair walked away from the shimmering shoreline. The rhythmic crunch of sand was a counterpoint to the frantic thump of his own heart. Palm fronds, ragged and bleached by the sun, clawed at the bruised sky. Blair's men, shadows clinging to the periphery, moved with the silent menace of predators.

"You made the right decision at the right time," Blair hissed, the words hanging in the air. An uncomfortable silence fell over the two men.

Hornigold fixed his gaze on the horizon, a bleak panorama of turquoise treachery. "Did I?" he rumbled, the question a low growl. Doubt, a venomous serpent, coiled in his gut.

The trail to the port was a sunbaked scar across the land, each step a slow burn of apprehension.

"You'll be after I tell you this!" Blair said, his voice tight with a nervous energy that vibrated in the humid air.

Blair stopped, turning to Hornigold, his eyes, the color of storm clouds, boring into the other man. "Remember Jolly Woodes Rogers?"

Hornigold swallowed hard. "Aye. Used to be one of us."

"Not so jolly anymore," Blair spat, the word tasting like bitter bile. "England's made him Captain-General- and Governor-in-Chief of our Bahama Islands." The emphasis was a venomous dart.

"Interesting," Hornigold murmured, but his eyes darted nervously towards the encroaching jungle.

"More interesting are the four warships of the Royal Navy he's bringing. To eliminate piracy in the West Indies. As if it were a simple... inconvenience." Hornigold's voice cracked, the weight of the news pressing down on him like a physical blow. He stopped dead, his body rigid with a sudden, chilling premonition.

"I don't think I want to remain here when that force arrives," he breathed, the words barely audible above the relentless whisper of the ocean.

A predatory smile, thin and cruel, stretched across Blair's face. "There's more," he purred, savoring the other man's unease. "A royal pardon for all pirates who surrender before September the fifth. All crimes forgiven."

Hornigold felt a cold dread creeping into his bones. "And?"

"An oath, of course. To renounce piracy forever." Blair leaned closer, a glint of something cold and calculating in his eyes. "Whatever you stole, whatever gold you've amassed...you keep it. A handsome offer, wouldn't you say?"

Hornigold laughed, a harsh, grating sound. "Handsome? Blair, you blind fool! What price do you think they'll demand for this... generosity?"

His voice rose, sharp as a broken bottle. "They'll want names! They'll want us to betray every man we've sailed alongside, every brother we've fought with! We'll be outlaws among outlaws, hunted by both sides! You save your own neck, but how many more will you condemn to the gallows!?"

The words fell hard, thick with accusation. Blair's face paled, the carefully constructed facade crumbling. The thought of betraying the pirate's code, of becoming a rat, etched itself across his features in stark lines of fear and self-loathing.

"Sweet Jesus..." Blair whispered, his voice choked with horror. "Our lives are forfeit!"

Hornigold clapped Blair on the shoulder, a surprisingly gentle touch. "Don't get your britches in a twist. Just be clever about this, lad. A game, that's all it is. A bloody dangerous game, but a game nonetheless." He nudged Blair forward, his gaze intense and unwavering. The fear remained, clinging to Blair like the relentless humidity.

"I didn't mean to give you such a fright," Hornigold said, his voice softer now, laced with an unsettling blend of weariness and calculation. "Warn an old man next time, mate. My heart can't take it." But the grim set of his jaw betrayed the lie. This was no mere fright; this was the terrifying dawn of a new, uncertain war.

Shifting Tides

The raucous cheers of the buccaneers, a guttural symphony of triumph, washed over the deck as Teach, Blackbeard himself, stalked towards Hornigold's quarters. The air, thick with the stench of salt, sweat, and rum, vibrated with anticipation. A rough hand clapped him on the back, a fleeting touch, yet carrying the weight of shared savagery. The lantern light glinted off the gold rings in his ears, highlighting the gleam in his eyes.

He knocked, the sound swallowed by the ship's groaning timbers. Inside, the cabin was a suffocating darkness, pierced only by the flickering candlelight that danced on Hornigold's face and the slivers of moonlight slicing through the grimy windows, illuminating the glint of a sliver-inlaid dagger at his hip. The air hung heavy with the cloying sweetness of spiced rum and the saturation of wet canvas and rope, a lingering scent from earlier spoils.

"You sent for me?" Teach's voice, a low growl that scraped against the silence.

Hornigold, grinning from ear to ear, his jowls quivering with barely controlled glee, gestured with a hand thick as a ship's hawser. "Aye. Sit."

A chilling silence descended, broken only by the rhythmic sloshing of rum in tankards. Teach felt the weight of the day on his shoulders. The unspoken question hanging heavy in the air... "What devilry have you wrought this time?"

"Did we bring hell with us today?" Teach's voice, laced with a hint of grim satisfaction.

Hornigold's grin widened, revealing teeth stained dark with wine and wickedness. "Aye. That we did." The words hung in the air, carrying the weight of their shared depravity.

Teach leaned forward, the candlelight catching the glint of a scar that snaked across his cheekbone, a map of past battles. "What is our prize? Or are there more than one?" His question dripped with anticipation, a predator circling its prey.

Hornigold poured a generous measure of rum; the amber liquid reflected the flames. His laughter was a rasping sound, born of years spent defying God and man. "The Concord. Sails from St. Malo. A prize indeed."

Teach nodded, a slow, deliberate movement. "Dutch built. Fast. They say she's heavily armed." He helped himself to a chunk of roasted meat, his gaze unwavering. The rich scent, so incongruous with the savagery of the night, did nothing to lessen the grim determination etched onto his face.

"When we broadsided her," Teach continued, his voice low and dangerous, "there was...no damage to her hull that I could see. Not a scratch." A subtle note of unease crept into the otherwise triumphant atmosphere. The silence that followed was far more unsettling than any boast.

"None." The word hung in the air, thick and heavy like salt air and spilled rum. "She can sail." That much was clear. "But what of her cargo?"

"The second prize? Ah, my boy. The glint of it still burns behind my eyelids. Gold, yes. Enough to pave a king's highway." Jewels that screamed obscenities of plundered empires, their fire a mockery of their victims' tears. Plates, gleaming under the dim light of the tavern, each piece a testament to avarice and brutal conquest. And money... mountains of it, enough to choke a miser's dreams. "A handsome sight, you say?" It was a feast for the eyes, a ship full of stolen wealth.

Teach swirled the liquor in his cup, the amber liquid catching the firelight like a trapped sun. The rough wood felt coarse against his calloused fingers; he tasted the sting of the rum and the bitter aftertaste of a thousand victories hard-won.

"Mighty handsome, I wager," Teach's voice, rasping like the groan of a ship's timbers in a storm, echoed in the suffocating silence. Hornigold leaned back, his shadow stretching long and malevolent across the rough-hewn floorboards. The air crackled between them, charged with unspoken ambitions and the stench of betrayal waiting just beneath the surface.

"Is there more, Teach? Or is there something festering behind that flint-hard gaze of yours? Spit it out, boy. Ask," Hornigold knows what's coming.

"I want her. The Concord." Her very timbers sang a siren song in Teach's blood. He wanted her speed, her power, the feel of her beneath his feet. More than that, Teach craved the freedom she represented, a freedom bought with blood and fire. "With your permission."

Hornigold's smile was a thin, cruel slash in the shadows. He knew the game, played it better than anyone. He saw the hunger in his eyes, the same dark hunger that burned within him.

"She's yours." Hornigold said with finality. " You've proven you can handle a ship of that size. And you know, my boy, some ships... are best handled alone."

Surprise was a luxury Teach couldn't afford, so he masked it. A slight twitch of his lips; a raising of the cup in acknowledgment. A silent toast to their shared depravity.

"Toast with me." Hornigold raises his tankard to meet Teach's.

The cups clinked; the sound was sharp and brittle. The rum never tasted so sweet.

"May all our days be as rich as today." Teach cracked a smile.

"We can only hope." The words were hollow, a lie spoken against the grim certainty of fate's inevitable reckoning.

 Hornigold's face, a bitter taste mirroring the gall rising in his throat. His gaze, drawn to the churning, grey expanse of the ocean, reflected a weariness deeper than any storm. The wind, a mournful keening, whipped through the rigging, a symphony of impending loss. "Now...what plagues that black heart of yours?" he rasped, turning to Teach, his voice rough as barnacles.

Hornigold's hand, gnarled and scarred, closed around the rum. The liquor burned a fiery path down, yet the chill in his bones persisted. "This night ends it, Teach. This life...this game... I've tasted the spoils, and the rot is setting in. I'll savor the sun before the darkness claims me." He downed the rest of the rum in one desperate gulp, the amber liquid gleaming like blood in the flickering lamplight. Teach's eyes widened, mirroring the sudden, stark terror in the confession.

"You...can't leave. This...it's you." Teach's voice, though low, vibrated with a raw, desperate energy.

Hornigold chuckled, a harsh, brittle sound. "A mystery, am I? You've always been too blind to see the cage. This...this glorious, bloody cage...it's built for men like you, a beast in human form. I'm... done. I've had enough of the stench of blood and the taste of fear."

Teach's fingers tightened into fists. "You'll just...walk away? Abandon it all?" The words were a strangled cry.

Hornigold rose, his silhouette a dark stain against the window. The ocean roared its approval of his decision. "The men respect you, Teach. They fear you. You're a predator born of the storm. What more need I say?"

He turned, his face etched with a mixture of bitter regret and weary resolve. "They call you Blackbeard. They whisper your name like a ghost story. They see your sails and they pray for mercy. Hell itself sails under your black flag, Teach. A fearsome legacy you've forged. And I...I'm weary of this life."

Teach rose, his face pale, his hand trembling. "What...what do I tell them?" his voice was a mere breath.

Hornigold's laugh cut through the heavy silence. "Tell them their captain's found an island where the rum flows like wine, and the sun shines like gold. Tell them Hornigold's taking his leave at New Providence tomorrow. A fatted pig, enjoying his last sunset."

A silence descended, thick and suffocating as the air in a sinking ship. Teach finally spoke, his voice barely audible. "It will never be the same without you."

Hornigold's laugh was devoid of humor. "Aye, Teach. I've had my run. Now it's yours. Own the storm."

A slow, almost reluctant smile played on Teach's lips. Their hands met in a firm, desperate clasp, a silent pact forged between two titans, between destiny and escape. Hornigold clapped Teach on the shoulder, the gesture surprisingly gentle. "Come. Let's face our...men." The unspoken understanding hung heavy in the air: the end of an era, and the beginning of another, far bloodier one. The rise of Blackbeard has come.

The salt-laced wind whipped around the Concord, a tangible thing against the weathered faces of Hornigold and Blackbeard's crew. Packed like sardines on the groaning deck, they were a sea of sweat and grime, their whispers a low, guttural hum, thick with anticipation. The air crackled; a palpable tension, the scent of brine and fear mingling with the cloying sweetness of rum. The heavy oak door of the captain's cabin creaked open, revealing not just Hornigold and Teach but the shadow of a momentous decision.

Hornigold, his one good eye gleaming like a shark's tooth, surveyed the restless mass, a cruel, knowing smile twisting his lips. A roar erupted from the ranks, a guttural beast of a question.

The cry ripped from a throat raw with impatience and dread, "What news, Captain?!"

Israel Hands, Teach's first mate, a mountain of a man whose tattooed skin seemed to writhe with restless energy, bellowed, silencing the mob with a roar of his own. "Quiet, you bilge rats!" His voice, a rasping growl, sent shivers down spines.

Hornigold stepped forward, the gleam in his eye intensifying. He paused, the silence heavy as a shroud, before his words cut through the oppressive air. "We've bled these waters crimson, lads! We've

plundered enough gold to sink a dozen galleons.
But... my time on this ship... is done."

The ensuing cacophony was deafening, a maelstrom
of shouts, curses, and desperate pleas. Hornigold
raised a calloused hand, silencing them with the
practiced authority of a lion tamer. "Fear not! You
have a captain worthy of your loyalty, a man you've
sailed beside these long months..."

A cheer, raw and primal, tore through the night. They
knew who he meant. Hornigold's hand shot up
again, cutting short their jubilation. "And worry not
for me! Should you need me, you'll find me sunk in
rum on some sun-drenched beach, entertaining a
wench with stories of our glorious plunder!"

Laughter, unrestrained and boisterous, rolled across
the deck, a wave crashing against the cliffs of their
anxiety. Hornigold, a flicker of something akin to
sadness in his eye, exchanged a look with Teach, a
silent acknowledgment of the weight of their
decision.

The bosun's bellow cut through the mirth. "To the
captain!" A thunderous chorus, a sea of voices rising
in a tidal wave of loyalty and... uncertainty echoed
the cry.

Teach, his face obscured by shadow, turned to his new crew. With a flick of his wrist, his cutlass flashed in the moonlight. "Raise the colors!"

Slowly, deliberately, the black flag ascended between the masts, a symbol of terror unfurling slowly, deliberately. The skull, its empty sockets seeming to gaze upon them with an eerie intelligence, clutched an hourglass, its sands slipping away, mirroring the fleeting nature of life itself; while a spear pierced a heart, a crimson stain blossoming against the black canvas.

Blackbeard had arrived.

For Hornigold, it was more than a transfer of power; it was a gut-wrenching farewell to a life spent chasing fortune and glory, a goodbye to a home he knew he would never see again. The weight of that realization hung heavier than any anchor.

Rogers' Gambit

The H.M.S. Delicia, a leviathan of oak and iron, sliced through the churning, jade-green waters, her formidable presence underscored by four grim warships of the British Royal Navy, all converging on the distant, sun-drenched shores of New Providence.

In the hushed confines of a stateroom, beneath the flickering lamplight that cast dancing shadows, Governor Rogers, a man etched by a lean severity, his crisp uniform a stark contrast to the sweat beading on his brow, knelt beside Captain David Messing. Messing, a monolith of a man, his frame bursting from the immaculate confines of his H.M.S. Rose uniform, his gaze sharp and unyielding. Beside them, Lieutenant Robert Moore, a sculpted figure in the polished brass and deep blue of the H.M.S. Milford, his handsome features taut with anticipation, all four heads bent over a sprawling chart of the Bahama Islands, its edges brittle with age.

Captain Messing's heavy hand, calloused from years of wielding a cutlass, settled upon the table. The polished wood groaned softly beneath the weight of their shared destiny.

"Thank you, gentlemen, for your prompt assembly," Governor Rogers 'voice, a low rumble, barely disturbing the tension that coiled in the air.

Captain Messing, his gaze never straying from the map, replied, his voice a deep baritone, "Is this a matter of grave urgency, Governor?"

"Indeed, Captain. We are but two days 'sail from the Caribbean's embrace."

"Yes, sir," Moore chimed in, his youthful voice surprisingly steady, "We should make New Providence precisely as scheduled."

A flicker of something unreadable, a ghost of a smile, played on Rogers 'lips, a smile that promised no comfort. "My concern, Captain, is not with our arrival. Your command is beyond question. My disquiet lies here." His finger, a skeletal digit, jabbed at a narrow sliver of blue on the map, a perilous strait nestled between the emerald shoulders of Abaco and Eleuthera. "Our final hundred miles, this gauntlet between Abaco and Eleuthera. This is where we will be exposed, Captain. Vulnerable."

Messing's chest expanded, a surge of confidence radiating from him. "Governor, I assure you, we have taken every precaution to ensure your passage is as secure as the King's own treasury."

Rogers 'eyes, sharp and piercing, met Messing's. "I pray you are correct, Captain. Make no mistake, the whispers of my governorship have already reached the Caribbean's shadowy corners. And there are many who would relish seeing this… military spectacle… falter in its purpose."

A low, rumbling chuckle escaped Messing's lips, a sound that seemed to grate against the confined space. "You speak of pirates, Governor?"

Rogers 'composure fractured, his voice cracking with an almost unbearable frustration. "Pirates! Yes, pirates! And your flippant tone, Captain, this damnable, ingrained arrogance of the British Royal Navy! I will never understand it! Why, tell me, do you believe Britain's efforts to eradicate this scourge have met with such pitiful failure?"

Messing, for the first time, appeared taken aback, his bluster faltering. "I… I confess I have no ready answer for you, sir."

"Precisely!" Rogers 'voice boomed, echoing in the small room. "Because you fail to grasp the sheer, unadulterated audacity of these men! They do not adhere to your protocols, Captain. They do not play by your rules." He fixed both officers with a gaze that seemed to bore into their very souls. "The reason I understand this so intimately," he confessed, the words laced with a raw, potent honesty, "is because for a time I was one of them. These men regard England's vaunted military strategies as nothing more than a child's diversion, a mere game of chess played with lives and destinies."

The polished mahogany of the war room seemed to absorb the stunned silence that fell between Captain Messing and Lieutenant Moore. Their eyes, twin pools reflecting the flickering lamplight, locked in a shared, unspoken tremor of disbelief. Messing's voice, when it finally cut through the heavy air, was a low rumble, laced with an edge that promised more than mere apology.

"Governor," he began, the title a gravelly whisper, "I assure you, I do not underestimate these men. But the steel forged within the hearts of our own… that is a force I would be a fool not to trust." The surrounding air seemed to crackle, a palpable tension emanating from the sheer force of his conviction.

Lieutenant Moore, a study in rigid resolve, snapped to attention. The creak of his boots on the flagstone floor was a sharp counterpoint to the coiled energy in his stance. His voice, when he spoke, was a whip crack, sharp and unyielding. "We shall amplify our vigilance tenfold as we traverse the serpent's coils of that island chain." His gaze, fixed on the Governor, burned with an almost predatory intensity, as if the very notion of danger ignited a hidden fire within him.

Messing's head swiveled, his attention now a honed blade directed at his second. "Precisely, Lieutenant. Make sure your men are as sharp as a razor. Every nerve singing with alertness. I will personally convey the word to the Buck and the Shark. Let them know the storm is coming." A grim satisfaction settled on his features, a predator anticipating the hunt.

Governor Rogers, a man whose every movement was a carefully curated performance, observed them both. A slow, knowing smile, subtle as the scent of gunpowder, graced his lips. The unspoken understanding, the raw efficacy of their promise, settled upon him like a warm cloak. "Gentlemen," he intoned, his voice smooth as aged whiskey, "your dedication is... appreciated. That will be all."

The two officers, a synchronized unit of coiled power, turned in unison. The heavy oak door beckoned, a gateway to the grim reality awaiting them. But as they reached its threshold, Rogers' voice, now a silken thread of command, snagged Messing.

"Captain."

Messing froze. The sound was a caress, but it held the sting of a lash. He turned, the movement slow, deliberate, like a coiled viper unfurling. His eyes, still sharp from the previous exchange, met Rogers.

"Yes, sir?"

A flicker of something akin to respect, or perhaps a shared understanding of the brutal game they played, danced in Rogers 'gaze. "I... have faith in you, Captain. And in the men who stand with you." The words, simple as they were, resonated with the weight of unspoken sacrifices, of battles fought and won.

A ghost of a smile touched Messing's lips, a fleeting acknowledgment of the Governor's rare vulnerability. "Thank you, sir." The words were clipped, professional, yet carried a subterranean current of shared purpose.

He turned again, the war room now a silent testament to the gravity of the moment. Governor Rogers remained, a solitary figure amidst the maps and stratagems, the lingering scent of lamp oil and anticipation clinging to the air. The weight of what was to come pressed down, a silent, heavy promise.

The Price of Infamy

The Queen Anne's Revenge, once the meek Concord, now cuts the waves under a taut, savage press of sail, a predator embracing the western end of Jamaica. Blackbeard, eager to take down his prey, hounds a Spanish galleon, its hull groaning towards the ill-fated promise of Port Royal. Hot on the Revenge's heels, a venomous shadow, sails The Avenger, his other sloop, their combined hunger a palpable force closing the distance. The galleon, a plump, oblivious prize, continues its stately progress, a feast for the eyes of the sharks closing in.

On deck, a frenzy of controlled chaos erupts. The metallic rasp of cutlasses being drawn, the thump of powder kegs being hefted, the ominous scrape of iron cannonballs rolling across the timber–these are the harbingers of doom. Blackbeard, a mountain of scarred leather and wild beard, strides the deck of the Queen Anne's Revenge, the very air around him thick with a primal energy. He surveys the feverish preparations, his gaze a burning brand. Israel Hands, his first mate, a man whose eyes held the glint of a thousand forgotten promises, glided through the men to stand beside him.

"We are ready, Captain," Hands rasped, his voice like grit on stone.

Blackbeard, his knuckles white on the helm, peers through a polished brass spyglass; the world reduced to a single, glittering prize. The unsuspecting crew of the galleon, a blur of routine motion, are utterly ignorant of the thunder that awaits them, the storm of righteous fury about to break.

"Good," Blackbeard breathes, a low rumble in his chest as the spyglass dips. He turns, a predatory gleam in his eyes, to his first mate. "Are you hungry, Israel?"

A slow, wicked grin split Hands 'face, revealing teeth that were rotten from rum and years of neglect. "Aye, Captain."

Blackbeard moves to the edge of the quarterdeck, his presence commanding silence. He bellows, his voice a guttural roar that slices through the salt-laced air, cutting through the clamor of preparation. "Are you men ready to take what is YOURS?"

A thunderous chorus answers him, a single, ravenous cry, "YES!" "And who needs it?" Blackbeard's voice cracks like a whip.

The response, a primal, unified surge of desire, explodes from the throats of every pirate on deck. "WE NEED IT!" The thirst for plunder, for victory, for the very taste of true freedom, is a hunger that the pirates will soon satisfy.

Blackbeard, ready to broadside the galleon, grips the ship's wheel, his knuckles white as bone. His guttural roar sliced through the gale, a primal decree "Now!"

From the shadows, a tide of savagery erupts. Pirates, coiled like vipers, sprang forth, their forms a jagged silhouette against the approaching galleon. A symphony of war cries, raw and bestial, tears from Blackbeard's crew, a chilling promise of the carnage to come. High above, a spectral banner, the embodiment of dread, unfurls to the mast's zenith, its black heart beating a furious rhythm against the wind.

Higgins, a man who always fixed his gaze on the horizon, now feels the very earth lurch beneath him. He sees the figures on the enemy decks surge upward, the dread ensign a death knell. Terror, cold and absolute, seizes him. The pirate behemoths are a suffocating vise; escape is a phantom limb.

"By the heavens!" he gasped, his voice a thin thread against the rising storm of fear. The first mate recoils, his eyes, wide and vacant as a drowned man's, betraying a soul already lost.

"Merciful God!"

A desperate shriek tears from Higgins's throat. He whirls, hands scrabbling for a grip on the polished wood of the staircase railing, his voice a frantic echo down to his cowering men "ARM YOURSELVES!" Passero, a shadow born of defiance, plunges down the steps, his boots slamming a desperate cadence on the main deck.

"Arm yourselves! Every scrap, every shard! Grab what you can!" His words were a volley of desperation. "We are under siege! There is no breath left to spare!"

"Charge the cannons!"

The Queen Anne's Revenge and The Avenger, predatory titans, have closed in, their immense hulls flanking the galleon like twin jaws of oblivion.

Higgins, a frantic moth drawn to a destructive flame, scans the chaos for Passero. His eyes locked onto the first mate, a flicker of desperate hope igniting within him. He lunges, his hand clamping onto Passero's arm with a strength born of sheer panic. "We must hold the line! We must maintain order!"

But the pandemonium swallowed his words. The crew, a stampede of terrified souls, surged around them, a human tide of confusion and despair.

Passero's voice, a raw, ragged cry, cuts through the cacophony. "Orders, Captain? What orders? Most of these men have never known the kiss of cold steel!"

And then, without preamble, the world exploded. Cannons roar, a thunderous maw of fire and iron, and the ship groans, a dying beast wracked by an agony beyond comprehension.

The groaning timbers of Higgins' vessel shrieked as two behemoths slammed into their flanks, a brutal, tearing embrace that threatened to splinter their very souls. A choking pall of acrid smoke, thick as a drowning man's last breath, billowed from the cannon muzzles, searing the eyes and filling the lungs. Higgins, his vision blurred by the stinging haze, strained to pierce the inferno. His gaze snagged on the enemy's broadside, a silhouette emerging from the chaos like a demon birthed from hellfire.

A devil of a man, swathed in shadows, his frame bristling with a deadly array of pistols, commanded the opposing deck. A beard, black as a moonless night and braided with wicked intent to its very ends, framed a face that seemed carved from obsidian. And then Higgins saw it. The man's beard appeared to be on fire, a living pyre against the smoke-choked backdrop; his form commanding, yet impossibly, impossibly still.

Higgins' breath hitched, his eyes widening into saucers of pure terror. A primal, guttural sound escaped his lips, choked and lost in the cacophony of battle. "My God!" he whispered, the words a desperate plea against an unfathomable reality.

An icy dread, a phantom hand, clamped around the captain's heart, squeezing the life out of him. "We have to do something!" The declaration was ripped from his chest, a raw, instinctive cry for survival, yet his limbs refused to obey. He stood frozen, a statue carved from dread, his gaze locked on the incandescent figure of Blackbeard, utterly mesmerized, his mind a battlefield of fear and disbelief.

Passero, his weathered face a mask of grim desperation, grabbed Higgins by his salt-stained shirt sleeve, his knuckles white. "CAPTAIN!" The shout was a lifeline, a desperate attempt to anchor his captain to this world of blood and fire. He shook him again, a frantic, soul-wrenching tremor, and then, with a final, desperate wrench, Passero released his grip. Higgins slumped, a broken thing, and fell to the deck, his body landing with a sickening thud, utterly lifeless.

Upon the stern of the Queen Anne's Revenge, Blackbeard stood as if rooted to the deck, an avatar of righteous fury. His men, like specters in the swirling smoke, hurled grappling hooks, their iron claws biting deep into the galleon's hull, dragging them closer, closer. The air thrummed with the relentless roar of cannon fire, punctuated by the sharp, staccato bark of pistols, each shot echoing against the encroaching vessels.

There was no escape. Passero knew it. Higgins knew it. A tide of snarling cutthroats, a tempest of steel and gunpowder, surged over the rails. Pistols spat fire and lead, a macabre dance of death ripping through the galleon's decks, targeting any flicker of defiance, any hint of movement. The merchant crew, their faces a mask of terror etched by the acrid sting of burnt powder, scrambled for their own meagre defenses. The guttural shouts of Blackbeard's brutes, a symphony of pure savagery, echoed as they carved their way through the panicked defenders, leaving a blood-soaked testament to their merciless brutality. They offered no quarter. They would not show mercy.

Amidst the carnage, Passero, his jaw set like flint, planted himself before Higgins, a living bulwark against the encroaching madness. They watched, paralyzed by the sheer overwhelming force, as the encroaching madness ripped their ship, their livelihood, and their very lives from their grasp. The futility of their struggle was a crushing weight, a swift, brutal realization dawning in the eyes of the galleon's crew. The odds were a cruel joke; Blackbeard's men a ravenous swarm. Defeat was a bitter draught, and many, their spirits broken, dropped to their knees, hands raised in desperate surrender.

Then, a figure of legend, a shadow carved from the very darkness of the sea, stepped onto the sea-soaked planks. Blackbeard, his cutlass gleaming like a sliver of hellfire in the dim light, his eyes burning with an infernal hunger, surveyed the scene. His men, a disciplined, terrifying legion, had herded the remaining crew into ragged lines, their pistols poised like venomous fangs, their swords held with intent. The air thrummed with a palpable dread, a suffocating silence that screamed of imminent judgment. For these merchant sailors, hell had landed aboard their ship.

Blackbeard's gaze, sharp as a shark's tooth, swept across the terror-stricken faces. "Where," his voice a gravelly growl, laced with the promise of unspeakable pain, "is the captain of this vessel?"

A lone voice, surprisingly steady, cut through the suffocating tension. "He is here."

Blackbeard's head snapped around, his piercing gaze locking onto the speaker. His eyes, dark as the deepest abyss, then fell upon a solitary figure standing tall, and another, seated with his back pressed against the sturdy mast, a silent sentinel. A cruel smile touched Blackbeard's lips as one of his hulking henchmen pressed the cold steel of a pistol against the temple of the seated man. With unnerving grace, Blackbeard advanced, the weight of his reputation preceding him. "Are you," he inquired, his voice dropping to a dangerous whisper that promised only oblivion, "the captain of this ship?"

A Legacy Born

Passero's head gave a subtle, almost imperceptible shift, his gaze dropping to the splintered deck, a silent summons to the man below. Blackbeard's shadow fell like a sudden storm. His head canted, a predator's assessment, as he moved, not merely approaching, but descending upon them. The gleam of his sword, a silver promise of torment, found Higgins.

"You there..." The voice, a gravelly growl that seemed to scrape against the salt-laced air, paused. "... are you the captain of this vessel?"

The blade, sharp and unyielding, bit into Higgins's shoulder, a stark punctuation mark against his huddled form. The cold steel, a tangible threat against the rough wool of his coat, sent a shiver that had nothing to do with the sea breeze.

"Speak up!"

Higgins, a knot of terror constricting his throat, could only nod. The very name "Blackbeard" was a phantom that stalked the whispers of every sailor, a legend etched in blood and fear. His breath hitched, a ragged sound lost in the rising wind.

Blackbeard's laughter was a harsh, barking sound, devoid of mirth. "What's wrong with you? Can't stand to face me?" His eyes, burning coals in the dim light, flicked upwards to Passero.

Passero's voice, strained but steady, a lifeline in the encroaching darkness, cut through the tension. "He's frightened."

"Frightened?" Blackbeard's gaze snapped back to Passero, a viper's focus. "And what of you?"

"Please," Passero pleaded, the desperation a raw ache in his tone, "just tell us what you want."

"I believe," Blackbeard purred, the silk of his words a chilling contrast to the steel in his hand, "we've already made that clear." He jabbed at Higgins once more; the impact sharp, the unspoken accusation a lash. "Your men have more courage than you!"

Blackbeard gestured to the pirate with a sweeping gesture, a silent command crackling with authority. "Pick him up."

The order was a chilling echo, swiftly obeyed. Higgins, a puppet on unseen strings, was hauled from the deck. Another brute, his face a mask of grim purpose, shoved Passero aside with brutal efficiency.

His rough hands finding Higgins's arm, a crude scaffold for the captain who still refused to meet Blackbeard's gaze. "Look at me!"

The demand was a physical blow. Blackbeard's hand, calloused and strong, clamped onto Higgins's jaw, his grip unyielding. He twisted Higgins's head, forcing his eyes upward into the fiery depths of his own.

"How can you be a captain of a ship like this," Blackbeard spat, the words dripping with contempt, "and be such a spineless bastard?"

A choked sob, a broken sound, tore from Higgins's throat. He wept, his body wracked with a terror so profound it was a palpable thing, a suffocating miasma that clung to them all.

"Have your fill, sir... just let my men go free." The captain's voice, a raw whisper choked with desperation, hung heavy in the dense, humid air.

With a brutal, explosive force, Blackbeard's fist connected with the captain's face. The sharp crack echoed, followed by the sickening thud as the man reeled back, blood blooming on his lip, a metallic tang now mingling with the brine.

"Your crew? I'd sooner drown them than suffer your kind breathing the same air! Men like you... you fester in the light!" Blackbeard's head snapped to the side, his eyes, dark as a sunless abyss, drilling into the captain.

"This is my price. My wager. Are you even capable of listening?"

Closing the distance, a predator closing in on wounded prey, Blackbeard's breath, hot and reeking of rum, ghosted against the captain's ear.

"I won't grant you the mercy of death. No, I'll brand you with a deeper wound. Every blackening night that falls, when you dare to close your eyes, and every blinding dawn that breaks... you will see me. You will know that your very existence, from this moment, is a stolen breath, a debt owed to me." His voice dropped to a guttural rasp, a promise more terrifying than any threat. "Do you understand?"

Blackbeard's presence receded, his shadow stretching long as he turned to address his own hardened crew, his voice a thunderclap.

"Pack these landlubbers into the longboats. Send them sputtering toward the shore. Unless-" a sly, dangerous glint danced in his eyes, "unless one of you craves a taste of true fortune, and fancies joining our ranks!"

He let the silence stretch, a palpable tension coiling among his men. No one moved. Not a single soul dared to step forward.

"Then so be it," Blackbeard's lips curled into a chilling smile. "Send them on their way to Jamaica. A fitting destination, I'd wager, for such a timid flock."

Israel's boots grated on the salt-slicked deck as he stalked towards Blackbeard. The atmosphere was thick with fear and the smoldering scent of gunpowder.

"And the captain?" Israel's voice, a low growl, scraped against the tension like barnacles on a hull.

Blackbeard, a monstrous silhouette against the bruised twilight sky, his beard a tangled storm of midnight, turned slowly. A cruel smile, sharp as a harpoon point, split his face. "The captain, you ask? Oh, he's going. Just... not in the comfort of a longboat." His gaze, burning like coals from a dying fire, flicked to the two hulking brutes holding Higgins captive. Higgins, limp as a gutted fish, dangled between them, his limbs askew, his very being a testament to utter helplessness.

"Toss this sniveling cur over the side," Blackbeard commanded, his voice a thunderclap that vibrated through the very timbers of the ship. "And when you do," his eyes gleamed with hunger, "throw him as hard as you can. I want his flesh to sting when he hits the water. Let him taste the ocean's fury before he drowns!"

A wave of dark, brutish energy surged through Blackbeard's crew. They moved with chilling efficiency, their rough hands hefting chests and crates from the galleon's belly, the heavy thud of wood against wood a counterpoint to the frantic scrabbling of those being forced into the longboats. Blackbeard's roar split the air, a warning laced with venom. "Any among you who dare to aid your captain will get a ball between the eyes! Today, you witness a lesson etched in blood and brine!"

Higgins, dragged like a sack of stolen plunder towards the ship's edge, began to thrash. A desperate, pathetic sound, a strangled whimper, escaped his lips. He clawed at his captors, his pleas a thin, reedy wail against the rising tide of chaos. "I can't... I can't..."

Blackbeard advanced, his massive frame eclipsing the dwindling light. "Can't what, Higgins?" he purred, the sweetness of his tone more terrifying than any roar. Higgins, his face a mask of pure, unadulterated terror, his eyes wide and darting between the impassive faces of his tormentors and the towering figure of Blackbeard, choked out his confession, his voice a raw, ragged whisper. "I... I can't swim very well."

Blackbeard's grin stretched across his face as he cocked his head, the movement unnerving in its deliberate menace.

"But you can swim?" He laughs devilishly.

With a guttural bark, Blackbeard gestured, and the two hulking pirates, their knuckles white, seized Higgins. The pirates yanked him, a strangled gasp torn from his throat, and with a sickening heave, flung him over the railing. The impact with the churning water was a brutal smack, a violent punctuation to his terror.

Blackbeard, unfazed, turned from the railing, his heavy boots echoing on the deck as he strode towards the growing pyre of chests and crates. His gaze landed on Israel, a silent command passing between them.

"Israel! Gather five men. You'll be plundering the very gut of this vessel for every grain of black powder. Stack it in the hold, double-time!"

A flicker of confusion crossed Israel's weathered face. "You... you don't want the ship, sir?"

Blackbeard's head snapped back, his eyes, the color of a storm-tossed sea, locking onto Israel's. A chilling amusement danced within them. "No. I want to tear her asunder. I want to watch her bottom erupt in a blaze of glory, a roaring inferno that sends a message. A message to the crew of this floating corpse will carry, screaming, all the way to the Governor of Port Royal!"

He drew a flintlock pistol, its polished metal glinting, and with a deafening BANG, he fired. The shot ripped through the air, shattering the lock of a nearby chest. With a rasp, he wrenched it open, revealing a cascade of gleaming silver plates and ornate golden goblets.

A low growl rumbled in Blackbeard's chest as he surveyed the bounty. "Ah, there's the sweetness I craved." He met Israel's gaze again, a gleam in his eyes. "Take all of this. Every last coin. To our own vessel."

"Aye, sir." The word was a breath of loyalty, tinged with the same ruthless ambition that fueled their captain.

On the shore, the tattered remnants of the galleon's crew huddled, their faces etched with a grim, salt-laced despair as they stared out at the roiling ocean. Passero stood by Higgins, as silent as the grave. Higgins, still shivering, water clinging to him like a second skin, the brutal swim a raw ache in his bones. Then, a thunderous CRACK ripped through the air, followed by a deep, guttural BOOM that vibrated through the very earth. The distant, crippled galleon shuddered. Without a breath of warning, another earth-shattering blast tore through the silence, culminating in a cataclysmic explosion. The men on shore threw themselves down, the air thick with the stench of gunpowder. Shards of splintered wood, like jagged teeth, rained down, streaking across the water. The ship's colossal mast, now a torch, erupted in flames, then toppled, crashing onto the doomed vessel. The magnificent galleon, once a proud queen of the seas, groaned in her death throes, slowly, inexorably, succumbing to the crushing embrace of the deep.

Passero turns to Higgins, his voice thick with a regret he can't quite mask. "I'm sorry, sir."

Higgins, his gaze fixed on the sinking wreckage, offers no response; his mind a storm of its own. The sheer futility of their struggle hangs heavy in the air, a bitter testament to a battle lost. He remembers the roar of the cannons, the splintering wood, the desperate cries–all now reduced to this mournful spectacle. Yet, even in defeat, a flicker of defiance remained. They stood their ground. And though the sea claims their vessel, it cannot claim their spirit.

Blackbeard sits at a table, alone, the flickering lantern light casting long, dancing shadows across the meticulously drawn maps. The cabin is a sanctuary of sorts, a stark contrast to the boisterous revelry of his crew on deck. The muffled sounds of drunken singing and raucous laughter serve as a distant, comforting hum. He takes a long drink from the bottle; the warmth spreading through him like a welcome tide. The day's victory was hard won, a symphony of thunder and steel, and the taste of success is as potent as the rum.

There's a knock on the door. "Come!" Blackbeard's voice was a low, growling tone.

The door opens, and Israel Hands enters, his face a mixture of exhaustion and anticipation. He placed his hand on the splintered wood of the doorframe.

"Captain. The men want to know if you will be joining them on deck." The room is still. Inviting. The aroma of whale oil from the cabin's lanterns filled the air.

Blackbeard glances up at Israel, a glint of amusement in his eyes. He savors the moment, letting the quiet contemplation wash over him. The adrenaline of the chase and the thrill of the engagement have subsided, leaving behind a satisfying weariness.

"Not tonight, Israel. I want some peace." Blackbeard runs his hand through his long, coarse beard. Silence was where his mind was.

"Aye, Captain." Israel paused before exiting the cabin, a question forming on his lips.

"Captain?" Israel placed his hand on the door frame of the cabin again. A splinter of wood finds its way into his palm. He tries hard not to wince.

"Yes?" Blackbeard doesn't shift his gaze. He remains sitting in his reflection of the day. The crew's sounds of celebration, although muffled, soothed his mind.

"Will we be making port soon?" Israel poses the question in a firm tone so as not to sound weak in the asking. "That depends." Blackbeard takes another drink. The rum dripped down his coarse beard. "On what, Captain?" Isreal's curiosity spirals.

"Whether you want a run-in with the British in Port Royal."

Israel pauses for a moment, the unspoken implication sinking in. The thought of facing the Crown's might after such a grueling day is hardly appealing.

"Not in particular." Blackbeard smiles back, a slow, knowing curve of his lips. He appreciates Israel's pragmatic thinking.

"I was looking forward to having the company of a woman and a pint of rum." Blackbeard slyly turned his head.

Israel nods in agreement, his own desires aligning perfectly with his captain's. The prospect of easing into port after a triumphant encounter, to bask in the rewards of their bravery, is a welcome thought.

"That sounds mighty fine, Captain." An inner sigh of relief washes over him. Unpredictability is something he's all too familiar with dealing with Blackbeard. You really never know what will come out of the man's mouth. If you're a man of acute anxiety, being part of his crew may not be the place for you. In fact, it isn't.

"Tortuga. We'll be spending the night in Tortuga."

A wave of relief and excitement washes over Israel's face. The men will feel elated. This victory, hard-fought and dearly bought, deserves a proper celebration. Blackbeard knew it. Understanding the temperament of his men was a hard-learned lesson from years at sea. Keep your men happy. Give them direction, a good meal here and there, a prize to take, and of course wenches and wine, and they will follow you to the ends of the mapped earth and beyond.

"I'll tell the men. They'll want to hear this news." A newfound energy takes hold.

"Leave me now." Blackbeard dismissively raises his hand. Every storm needs a calm. This was his. These fleeting evenings where everything is perfect. Every moment savored. Because they won't come again.

Jolly Woodes Rogers

Governor Rogers, a shadow cast long against the unforgiving sun, emerged from the suffocating confines of his stateroom; the polished brass of the railing biting into his palm as he stepped onto the heaving deck. Beside him, Captain Messing, a man whose weathered face spoke of a thousand storms weathered and won, radiated an unnerving calm, his gaze fixed on the horizon. The air thrummed with the frantic dance of canvas and rope as the crew wrestled with the sails, a symphony of taut lines and snapping fabric. Their destination. Achieved. Messing's voice, a low rumble, broke the tension.

"On schedule, Governor. And not a whisper of rogue sails or cutlasses met. A clean passage." He offered a smile, a thin, sharp thing that didn't quite reach his unnervingly bright eyes.

Rogers turned, his own expression unreadable, a mask of carefully curated indifference. "As it should be, Captain."

Messing raised a spyglass, the polished lens glinting. His hand, usually so steady, trembled slightly as he lowered the instrument. His eyes, wide and stark against his tanned skin, locked onto Rogers. "My God. The beach… it's a seething mass. Hundreds. Armed to the teeth. We must prepare a boarding party." He made to move, the primal instinct for defense surging.

Rogers's hand, surprisingly strong, clamped down on Messing's arm, a gesture of absolute authority that radiated a chilling stillness. "Haste, Captain, is the thief of all advantage. We arm ourselves not."

Messing, a seasoned warrior utterly bewildered, stammered, "Not? But Governor, the threat—"

"That," Rogers interrupted, his voice dropping to a whisper that carried the weight of destiny, "is merely our welcoming committee. Stand down, Captain. All is as it should be."

On the distant shore, a tableau of chilling intent unfolded. Hornigold and Blair, their faces etched with a predatory stillness, stood flanked by a formidable contingent of three hundred men, their "former" pirate affiliations hanging in the air like the salt spray. Four imposing British Navy warships, their cannons bristling like a metallic forest, prowled the bay, their shadows stretching across the water. Longboats, brimming with officers whose expressions ranged from grim resolve to disquieting curiosity, churned towards the beach. And among them, a figure of authority, Governor Rogers, his gaze already fixed on the figures awaiting him. Hornigold and Blair, a study in coiled energy, stood side-by-side; their anticipation a palpable force.

"I trust this little gathering," Blair's voice, laced with a silken danger, cut through the murmur of the approaching fleet, "won't be overly... untidy."

Hornigold's lips curved into a slow, enigmatic smile that promised more than it revealed. "Untidy? My dear Blair, consider the implications. Three hundred hardened souls, poised like serpents, while a Governor and the King's Navy sail into their embrace. A most... interesting confluence of loyalties, wouldn't you agree?" The unspoken question remains, a promise of intrigue, of power, and perhaps, of a most unexpected reckoning.

To the Code

Blair recoils, a sharp gasp snagging in his throat, the air suddenly thick with unspoken threat.

"I understand now."

From the churning mass of bodies, a titan emerged: Charles Vane. A man etched by a thousand storms, his frame a testament to brutal survival, he moved with the predatory grace of a wolf. His shadow fell over Hornigold as he closed the distance, the roar of the surf and the frantic scramble of men barely registering the intrusion.

"Captain Hornigold." The voice was a low rumble, like stones grinding together.

Hornigold's gaze, sharp as a splintered mast, flicked towards Vane. "Aye."

"We've been speaking," Vane continued, his eyes, twin shards of blue ice, bore into Hornigold's. "Since your return. The men. They want you to be our voice."

A tremor ran through Hornigold, not of fear, but of something far more potent–a sudden, electrifying awareness of his own suddenly elevated status. The weight of it settled upon him, heavy and dark. "You… you speak of me?" he stammered, disbelief coloring his tone.

Vane's lips curled into a slow, unnerving smile, a predator's promise. "We trust you, Captain. We know you'll not betray the code."

Hornigold straightened, the surprise giving way to a fierce, unyielding resolve. The salt spray on his face felt like a baptism. "You have my word. I will see justice done. For all of us."

Vane's nod was a curt, sharp movement. Then, with a deliberate slowness that sent a prickle of ice down Hornigold's spine, Vane raised his pistol. The polished steel glinted, reflecting the harsh, unforgiving light. He brought the barrel up, not menacingly, but as an offering, a silent toast.

"To the code."

The words were resolute, a sacred oath. Hornigold met his gaze, the unspoken understanding passing between them like a spark igniting dry tinder. "To the code."

Vane turned then, melting back into the throng as if he'd been a phantom conjured from the very sea mist. Hornigold's attention snapped back to Blair, his expression unreadable. "Did you orchestrate this?"

"Not I," Blair replied, his voice thin, the shock still clinging to him.

On the shore, a silent, terrifying transformation began. The pirates, a wild, unkempt sea of faces, began to separate, to array themselves. Two long, stark lines formed, stretching from the very edge of the churning waves to the dark, looming maw of the fort behind them. The air crackled with an anticipation that was both thrilling and deeply unnerving.

The hulking longboats cutting through the choppy grey water transported Governor Rogers and his entourage of officers in crimson coats. As they beached with a groan of stressed timber, the salt spray, thick with the stench of tar and anticipation, kissed their grim faces. The shore, packed tight with a sea of rough faces and glinting cutlasses, parted like a wound as the officers began their march. The air thrummed with a coiled energy, a palpable tension that vibrated from the very cobblestones beneath their polished boots.

Front and center, a beacon of authority amidst the roughneck tide, strode Governor Rogers. His gaze, sharp and assessing, swept over the assembled rogues. Then, a thunderclap ripped through the charged silence. Every single pirate, a living wall of defiance, raised their pistols skyward. A deafening volley erupted, a guttural roar of defiance and grim acceptance, the acrid bite of gunpowder stinging nostrils and burning the eyes. The air vibrated with the sheer force of it.

As the last echo faded, the massive fort gates, iron teeth gnashing at the sky, slammed shut, sealing the dignitaries within. Two stony-faced British guards, their bayonets gleaming like slivers of ice, stood sentinel, unblinking sentinels against the roiling unrest outside.

The mass of pirates, a restless ocean now that the formalities were over, began to eddy and swirl, dissolving back into the shadows and smoky taverns from whence they came. Only Hornigold and Blair lingered, two wolves separate from the pack, their stillness a stark contrast to the surrounding commotion.

"Well, that be that then. Another page turned in this damned ledger." Blair runs his hands through his greasy, thinning hair.

Hornigold's eyes, sharp as a hawk's, scanned the milling throng, a restless search for a familiar, dangerous face. Vane was nowhere to be seen.

"Aye, it be that. But the real game, my friend, has only just begun."

Blair tilted his head, his gaze locking with Hornigold's, a flicker of something akin to unease, or perhaps grudging respect, in his own weathered eyes.

"Game? You call this...a game?" The sudden clarity of it all, of the day, falls on his shoulders.

A humorless smile, a glint of cunning in his depths, stretched across Hornigold's face. "I have the unenviable task, Blair, of convincing our esteemed Governor that the salt and blood have finally been washed from our veins. That we are no longer the scourge of these seas. A task, I dare say, as likely as teaching a shark to knit. But one, mind you, that must be undertaken, lest this 'game' turn to a very different kind of finality for us all."

The Devil You Know

The stench of salt, decay, and something indefinably foul assaulted the nostrils as the shadowy streets of Tortuga revealed itself. This festering cesspool, a haven for the desperate and the damned, pulsed with the illicit heartbeat of pirates, rumrunners, and smugglers. The Queen Anne's Revenge disgorged its grim cargo as Blackbeard, a titan carved from storms and shadow, strode ashore, his fearsome presence a palpable wave washing over the wharf.

As his crew, a motley legion of hardened ruffians, surged into the town square, a cacophony of raw revelry erupted. The raucous strains of a fiddle, sharp and drunken, warred with the guttural shouts of men pursuing terrified women, their laughter a desperate, shrill sound. The very air vibrated with the uncontrolled energy of rampant intoxication, the reek of spilled rum thick and cloying.

Blackbeard, surveying the town he knew well, raised a hand, a gesture that silenced the immediate frenzy. His voice, a gravelly rumble that promised both dominion and destruction, boomed, "This cesspit, tonight... it is YOURS, you dogs!" No truer words had ever been spoken to such a motley crew of men.

A deafening roar answered, a primal exultation that mingled with lewd catcalls aimed at the huddled lines of prostitutes, their painted smiles brittle against the harsh reality of their trade. The square became a feeding ground, a canvas of depravity, and it was for the taking.

"Tonight," Blackbeard continued, his eyes, dark as the abyss, sweeping over his men, "you take what you desire. But remember this: dawn breaks at first light. Any soul not back upon the Revenge will find themselves marooned on a forgotten shore. Consider yourselves warned."

Among the throng, the Bosun, a squat, barrel-chested brute whose sweat-stained shirt hinted at a lifetime of hard living, nudged the Steersman, a man whose face was a roadmap of sea-battered voyages. Their gaze fixed on a cluster of women before the Inn, their eyes–one a glinting shard of obsidian, the other a weathered sea-grey–locking in silent, brutal understanding.

"I fancy one of those," the Bosun grunted, the words rough as barnacles.

The steersman, a slow, knowing smirk spreading across his weathered features, leaned in, a conspiratorial whisper laced with a predatory edge. "Aye, you could take both of them if you had the stomach for it, you greedy dog."

The bosun's craggy face broke into a grin, a flash of broken teeth. "Aye, that's precisely what I was contemplating, my friend."

With the unspoken pact sealed, Blackbeard's men dispersed, a tide of hungry wolves unleashed upon a helpless flock, their boisterous energy echoing the frantic joy of children in a forbidden playground. Blackbeard himself, his gaze sharp and assessing, spotted the flickering, inviting glow of The Rogue, a familiar haunt. Israel Hands, a man whose scarred hands spoke volumes of his violent past, materialized beside him, a silent shadow. Together, they disappeared into the smoky embrace of the pub; the night promising more than just oblivion.

The heavy oak door groaned open, spilling the salty tang of the sea and the pungent reek of stale ale into the night. Inside, a cacophony of raucous laughter, guttural curses, and the clatter of tankards hammered the air. This was no common tavern; it was a den of vipers, a breeding ground for buccaneers, where freebooters with eyes as sharp as cutlasses and rum runners with secrets etched into their weathered faces nursed their libations.

Then, a shadow fell across the threshold. Edward Teach, known to the world as Blackbeard, strode in, Israel at his side. The very air seemed to crackle with his presence. A hush fell, a predator's stillness.

Dozens of hardened eyes, accustomed to the glint of steel and the spray of blood, snapped toward him. They knew. Oh, they knew who this monstrous legend was. A primal fear, tinged with a grudging awe, rippled through the room. Blackbeard's gaze, a predatory gleam, swept the room before locking onto the bartender–a hulking brute with hands like blacksmith's hammers, who visibly straightened behind the scarred counter.

The bartender's voice, rough as barnacles, rasped, "The usual, Captain?" A pregnant pause hung heavy, laced with anticipation.

Blackbeard's lips curled into a predatory smile, a flash of yellowed teeth in the flickering lamplight. "Rum it shall be!" he boomed, his voice a gravelly thunderclap that vibrated in the very bones of the pub.

The bartender, with a practiced, almost reverent motion, filled a thick, chipped mug with dark, potent rum. The amber liquid sloshed, promising oblivion and fire. As it settled before Blackbeard, he didn't reach for it. Instead, with a deliberate, unnerving slowness, he drew forth his powder flask. The metallic rasp of the stopper being removed, cut through the remaining murmur. With a practiced flick of his wrist, a dark cascade of gunpowder dusted the surface of the rum. A collective intake of breath. Blackbeard then produced a flint and steel. The sharp scrape echoed, a spark ignited, a tiny star born in the gloom, and he tossed it.

The mug detonated. A searing inferno erupted, a violent bloom of crimson and gold that momentarily bleached the faces of every soul present. The roar was deafening, a guttural exhalation of pure, untamed power. The flames consumed the liquid, the glass itself seeming to writhe under their fury. Then, as abruptly as it began, the conflagration died, leaving only the acrid bite of burnt powder and the lingering heat. Blackbeard snatched the still-smoking mug, the glass impossibly hot to the touch, and with a savage tilt of his head, drained the fiery, rum-soaked powder. The raw, burning liquid seared his throat, a testament to his godlike tolerance.

A wave of primal exhilaration surged through the pub. Tankards slammed against tables, voices roared in a unified chorus of primal approval, a salute to the man who danced with death and spat in its face.

"There's not a man in the lot of you who's brave enough to try my drink!" Blackbeard bellowed, his eyes blazing with a manic, unholy light, challenging each and every soul in the room. The men responded with a renewed, thunderous cheer, their fear momentarily eclipsed by the sheer audacity of his display.

Israel, watching the spectacle unfold, a grim fascination twisting his features, shook his head, an indistinct murmur escaping his lips, "Edward, your madness... it grows with every damned drop."

Blackbeard let out a harsh, rasping laugh, the sound like stones grinding together. "It merely adds a certain... je ne sais quoi."

Blackbeard's gaze, sharp as a cutlass, sweeps across the raucous den of the pub. Laughter fills the air. The nefarious lot, deep in conversation, left Blackbeard to his own vices. It was time to leave. He turns to Israel, his eyes holding a depth of unspoken commands.

"I think I'll take my leave." The words were a low growl, laced with an edge that brooks no argument.

Israel's head snaps up, a flicker of unease betraying his gruff exterior. "Where are you off to?"

"Don't worry yourself about it," Blackbeard replies, his voice a rumble that seems to vibrate through the very timbers of the pub. "I'll see you at the docks tomorrow morning." A potent blend of promise and veiled threat.

"Whatever you say, sir." The difference in Israel's tone is almost a tremor.

Blackbeard strides out, the heavy thud of his boots
echoing on the slick, mud-churned streets. The
biting sea air whips around him, carrying the salty
tang of brine and the distant cry of gulls. He melts
into an alleyway, a vortex of shadow, towards a
cluster of weathered cottages that huddle against
the relentless wind. From the inky blackness of a
recessed doorway, Jackson, a man so gaunt his bones
seem to strain against his skin, materializes. He's a
wraith, a shadow within shadows, and he begins his
silent pursuit, his steps unnervingly light. Jackson
trails Blackbeard, a hunter of secrets, keeping just
enough distance to gauge the predator's path, his
every movement economical, precise.

Blackbeard arrives at a small cottage, its windows
dark and uninviting. He pauses, a colossal silhouette
against the flickering torchlight, and spins around,
his senses on high alert, probing the darkness for
any telltale sign of observation.

Jackson, a living embodiment of the night itself,
presses himself deeper into the encroaching gloom,
his eyes, sharp and calculating, fixed on Blackbeard.

A heavy, resonant knock cracks the silence. A
moment passes, then another, each one stretching
taut with anticipation. The door creaked open,
revealing Maria. She is a vision, a splash of defiant
fire against the muted backdrop–her Spanish blood a

vibrant contrast to the grim surroundings. Her eyes widen impossibly as she beholds Blackbeard. With a guttural cry, a sound torn from the very core of her being, she launched herself into his arms, her embrace desperate, all-consuming.

"You're back." Her voice is a husky whisper, thick with a yearning that has clearly gnawed at her.

Blackbeard's lips curve into a smile that barely reaches his eyes, a smile that hints at both danger and a profound, possessive tenderness. "Aye, love! I am!"

Maria pulls back, her hands still clinging to his rough-spun coat, her gaze searching his face, hungry for truth. "For how long?"

"Just for tonight." The words, though soft, carry the weight of inevitability, a familiar ache.

Maria turns, her movements a liquid dance, and leads Blackbeard into the cottage. The warmth inside, a stark contrast to the biting wind, wrapped around them. A faint aroma of spices and wood smoke drifts out.

"Why is it always one night?" Her question hangs in the air, laced with a melancholy that Blackbeard seems to understand all too well.

"That be the life of a sailor, love!" His voice is a rough caress, a resigned acceptance of the sea's cruel demands.

As the door swings shut, muffling their voices, Jackson slinks from the shadows. He moves with the stealth of a predator, his lean frame folding itself into a crouch just outside the cottage, a silent sentinel at the threshold of their stolen moment. Inside, the joyous peal of Blackbeard's laughter, a surprisingly boisterous sound, erupts, mingled with Maria's answering mirth, a melody of reunion played out in the heart of the unforgiving night.

The Ruthless Pursuit

Blackbeard was a man of a thousand whispers; his wives scattered like fallen leaves in every port: thirteen, the rumors were. Thirteen souls tethered to his roguish charm. In truth, there were only seven, a mere glimpse into the labyrinth of his heart, a truth buried beneath the polished veneer that most were content to admire.

The morning arrived quickly. It's as though the previous night never happened. And as the first light of dawn crept in, a jarring CRASH of wood against wood ripped Jackson from his slumber. Instinct, honed by countless nights of fear, sent him scrambling into the thorny embrace of the underbrush. A shadow detached itself from the chaos–Blackbeard, his silhouette a stark accusation against the dawn. He strode with an unnerving purpose towards the water's edge, a predator surveying his domain. Jackson, skin slick with dew and dirt, followed, drawn by an irresistible, terrifying gravity.

The scent of salt and brine filled his nostrils as he crept towards the imposing hulls of the Queen Anne's Revenge and the Avenger. He melted into the grimy shadows behind a mountain of splintered barrels, the rough wood a welcome rasp against his cheek.

Blackbeard and Israel, a diabolical duo, navigated the creaking planks of the dock. Their booming voices cut through the morning mist as they tallied their motley crew. Then, Blackbeard's gaze snagged on his steersman and bosun, teetering like drunken specters, their strength leached away by the night's excesses.

A slow, predatory smile stretched across Blackbeard's lips, a terrifying bloom of amusement. "Looks like you two had a... spirited evening."

The bosun, his breath still thick with ale and the cloying aroma of cheap perfume, managed a choked grin. His skin bore the stark, crimson testimony of a woman's nails, his linen shirt a chaotic tapestry of lipstick stains. "Aye. Maybe too spirited, Cap'n."

Blackbeard's voice, a thunderclap that rippled across the water, commanded attention. "Load up, you sea dogs! The horizon calls, and a world of islands awaits our touch!"

A wave of bodies, some stumbling, some dragging their feet, surged up the gangplanks. Blackbeard and Israel watched them go, their expressions unreadable, two ancient gods observing the toil of lesser mortals.

Jackson, a phantom in their wake, tracked their movements until the last soul had vanished into the ship's underbelly. Then, he rose, a coiled spring, and bolted for the town square. Livestock ambled placidly amidst the lingering wreckage of the night–sprawled forms, their snores a guttural symphony.

He darted into a narrow alley, the stench of stale refuse and something far fouler clinging to the air. He stopped at a weathered door, his knuckles rapping a precise, urgent rhythm–a secret language whispered in the dark. His eyes, sharp and darting, scanned both ends of the passage, ensuring he was unobserved. The door swung open.

A man emerged, impeccably dressed in a dark navy coat and tan breeches, his presence radiating an almost alien order. A pristine white wig framed a face that was a study in calculated caution, topped by the sharp angles of a tricorn hat. He surveyed the alley with the keenness of a hawk, then turned his piercing gaze upon Jackson.

"Were you followed?" The well-dressed man's voice was a silken rasp, laced with an edge of steel.

"No, sir," Jackson's voice was a low rumble, heavy with unspoken burdens.

The man leaned closer, his eyes boring into Jackson's. "Report."

"Last night, I was coiled in the shadows, a phantom myself, when the impossible materialized. A hulking silhouette, a storm made flesh–Blackbeard." Jackson's movements are exaggerated. He raised his arms above his head to show the sheer size of the man.

The British spy, a man carved from suspicion and laced with nerves, his eyes–once sharp as a honed rapier–widened, saucers of sheer, unadulterated terror. The very air around him seemed to crackle with dread.

"Blackbeard. Here?" The words escaped him, a strangled gasp; his eyes moved frantically, instantly swallowed by the cavernous silence of the room. His voice dropped, a nervous whisper that made his face grow cold.

"Why didn't you come tearing to me the instant your eyes fell upon him?" The spy's grip, rough as barnacles, seized Jackson's worn shirt, pulling him close, their faces inches apart. The scent of stale ale and desperation hung heavy between them.

Jackson, his own voice a rough rasp, fought for breath. "I... I had to be certain." His heart racing as he desperately tries to explain his method.

The Brit's knuckles turned white, his grip tightening, a vise of desperate inquiry. "I shadowed him. Through the murky dawn, down to the slick, reeking docks." The grit of his teeth was a grinding, a furious engine of anxiety.

"And? What news did you glean from his whispers?" The seriousness of the situation weighs on him.

"Little," Jackson admitted, the word a bitter taste. "Only the echo of islands... a phantom destination. I strained my ears, but the wind snatched the rest, leaving only fragments."

The Brit's hold slackened, a weary surrender. His shoulders slumped, the weight of the unknown crushing him. "So, no compass. No direction. We are adrift in his wake, blind to his ultimate port?"

"I am... regrettably unable to provide more, sir." A silence followed. Dead end.

A tremor ran through the Brit. He fumbled in his pocket, producing four tarnished shillings; the glint of the metal was a meager consolation. He pressed them into Jackson's palm, his touch surprisingly cool. "Here. A meager payment for this... this shadow of intelligence. And more than you've earned, you whelp! Now vanish! Melt back into the filth before your very breath betrays us both!"

Jackson's ragged breaths tore through the suffocating gloom of the alley, each desperate stumble a testament to the primal fear clawing at his throat. The British spy, a man of icy control, watched from the alley's darkness, a delicate handkerchief emerging from his tailored pocket. The gesture was not one of sympathy, but of visceral revulsion as he meticulously wiped his hand, a silent declaration of the taint Jackson represented.

Miles away, under the blistering Bahamian sun, a different kind of tension coiled. Hornigold, ready for the worst outcome, stood sentinel outside Governor Rogers 'opulent office, a shadow beside the governor's perpetually flustered secretary. Two crimson-clad soldiers, their bayonets glinting like predatory teeth, guarded the threshold. Hornigold's knuckles, rough as a millstone, rapped a sharp, impatient tattoo against the heavy oak.

A voice, muffled by the thick wood, boomed from within, laced with an authority that vibrated in the very air. "Enter!" The secretary, his face a mask of practiced deference, pushed the door inward. A wave of stifling air, heavy with the scent of aged parchment and expensive cigar smoke, washed over them. He cleared his throat, the sound a pathetic tremor against the room's gravitas.

"Good day, sir. There is a Benjamin Hornigold here to… plead his case."

A man whose very presence seemed to drain the color from the room, Governor Rogers, hunched over his desk and scratched his quill with ferocious intensity across a stack of documents. He didn't look up, merely raised a manicured hand, a dismissive flick of his wrist that spoke volumes. "Send him in."

Rogers continued his furious scribbling, the scratching of his quill a frantic heartbeat in the suffocating silence. Hornigold's heavy boots crunched on the polished floorboards, the sound echoing the unshakeable resolve etched onto his face. Rogers finally lifted his gaze, his eyes, sharp as shards of glass, fixing on the pirate.

"It seems your… brethren have seen fit to thrust the burden of representation upon your shoulders."

He leaned back, the springs of his plush chair groaning in protest, a stark contrast to Hornigold's stoic presence. "A rather colossal undertaking, wouldn't you agree?"

A flicker of amusement, predatory and deep, played on Hornigold's lips. He clutched his battered hat, his knuckles white.

"May I… impose upon your hospitality?" Rogers inclined his head, a subtle gesture that acknowledged Hornigold's audacious intrusion. "By all means." He knows the game is set.

Hornigold lowered himself into an ornate fauteuil, its velvet worn smooth by generations of power. The antique wood groaned a mournful protest beneath his weight, a symphony of the old world yielding to the new. He settled, his gaze unwavering, a tempest held captive.

"Honestly, sir, I'm as perplexed as you are as to why I've been chosen to speak for every scoundrel on this godforsaken island."

Rogers laid down his quill, the sharp click of its nib against the inkwell a punctuation mark of immense weight.

"Perhaps," he drawled, his voice a silken thread woven with menace, "it is because you are, at your core... a pirate."

The word hung in the air, a brand. "Former," sir. The sea has tempered me, but it has not broken my spirit." Rogers allowed a slow, chilling smile to spread across his lips, a smile that promised both salvation and damnation.

"That, Mr. Hornigold," he purred, "remains to be seen. For I bring with me from England these."

He gestured to a thick sheaf of documents, their vellum brittle and yellowed with age.

"These will grant a pardon to any soul who has, in their time, trafficked in piracy. However," his voice dropped, a venomous whisper, "the contract is clear. They will hunt you if you or any of your pardoned group dare to commit even one act of piracy while under this grace. Hunted like the vermin you are, and hanged until your very souls are ripped from your bodies!"

He leaned forward, his eyes locking with Hornigold's; the intensity was a palpable force.

"It's a simple proposition, wouldn't you agree?" Rogers stares through Hornigold like a pane of glass. There was no other choice. Play by the rules or die. A ghost of a smile touched Hornigold's lips, a dangerous glint in his sea-worn eyes.

"Where," he asked, his voice low and steady, "do I sign?"

Rogers chuckled, a dry, rasping sound.

"Not yet, Mr. Hornigold. Patience is a virtue I suspect you've rarely indulged. I shall dispatch riders. Let word spread like wildfire: any pirate who craves absolution will find it here, within the hallowed walls of Fort William. I intend to grant this cleansing... en masse. Do we understand each other?"

Hornigold's nod was as solid and unyielding as the stone beneath his feet. The unspoken understanding between the governor and the pirate crackled in the air, a dangerous and stoic accord. The line in the sand has been drawn.

The Tide Turns

"I understand." The words hung in the air, a chill seeping into the room as Rogers rose, a statue of unwavering resolve and power. He moved with an unnerving stillness, circling his desk to stand before Hornigold, his shadow lengthening across the worn floorboards. The scent of stale pipe tobacco, usually a comforting presence, now felt thick and suffocating.

"I require a service, Hornigold." Rogers' voice was low, a rumble that vibrated not just in the ears, but in the very bones. It was a voice accustomed to command, honed by the salty spray of distant seas and the cold calculation of power.

Hornigold flinched, his gaze darting towards Rogers, a primal fear tightening his chest, an icy knot of dread blooming in his gut. The ornate tapestry behind Rogers seemed to writhe, the embroidered ships appearing to thrash in writhing storms. "Whatever it is, Governor... I am yours." The plea was barely a whisper, a fragile bird trapped in a gale.

"I need you to hunt." Rogers 'eyes, honed with ambition, pinned Hornigold. "To track down a few vermin who have dared to stain the Caribbean with their presence. New Providence, in particular, is a festering wound I intend to cauterize." He savored the metaphor, the slight curl of his lip betraying a hidden amusement that sent shivers down Hornigold's spine.

Hornigold swallowed; the rough fabric of his collar suddenly abrasive against his raw throat. His mind raced, a desperate hope flickering that the name he dreaded, the one that still tasted like ash in his mouth, would remain unspoken.

"Do you have their names?" Hornigold managed, his voice strained.

Rogers turned, a slow, deliberate movement, and his fingers, long and surprisingly delicate, sifted through a chaotic stack of parchment. The rustle of paper was amplified; each crisp edge a potential threat. The air grew heavy with anticipation, charged with an unseen energy. He paused, his hand hovering over a particular document, and a flicker of something unreadable crossed his face.

"Ah, yes. The ledger of the damned." Rogers 'voice took on a gravelly edge as he drew out a single, crinkled sheet. "Two scoundrels I wish delivered to my presence, Hornigold. Two men who have carved their reputations with blood and bone." He began to read, his voice a low drone that seemed to suck the warmth from the room.

"A Christopher Condent. And a Charles Vane."

Hornigold's breath hitched, a strangled gasp that barely escaped his lips. The names were like the sting of a viper's fangs. He squeezed his eyes shut for a fraction of a second, the image of a particular swagger, a particular glint of defiance, searing itself behind his eyelids. When he opened them, he fixed his gaze on Rogers, his face etched with a desperate plea.

"Governor," he began, his voice a raw rasp. "May I... venture a question?"

Rogers' gaze, sharp and unwavering, met his. "Speak freely, Hornigold. Unless you fear the answer." The challenge was subtle, a flick of a mental whip.

"Why... why me, Governor?" The question was out; a leap into the abyss. "Why am I the instrument of your... displeasure?"

A slow, almost gleeful smile spread across Roger's face. He leaned forward, his voice dropping to a near whisper that still carried the weight of authority. "Because, Hornigold," he purred, the sound like the rasp of a cat's tongue against raw meat, "any band of pirates who elevate a single man to speak for their collective depravity... they must, by necessity, possess the knowledge. The knowledge of how and where to unearth their brethren. You know the shadows, Hornigold. You know the currents that carry them. And that, my friend, is precisely why I have need of you."

Hornigold's gaze, sharp as a shard of sea-glass, snaps upward to meet Rogers' own. The air in the dimly lit room crackled, thick with the brine of the ocean and the unspoken weight of past deeds.

"You are right about that, Governor," Hornigold rasps, his voice like grit grinding against rock. "Tell me something, Governor, did you find it difficult to pry yourself from this life? To shed the salt and the savagery like a snake sheds its skin?"

For a moment, the two men don't move a muscle. They continue to weigh and measure each other. The silence stretches, taut as a straining rope, before the Governor finally speaks, his voice a low rumble that seems to vibrate the very timbers of the room.

"Do you find any... problems," Rogers muses, the word laced with a subtle, dangerous edge, "in what I've asked you to do?"

Hornigold's jaw tightens, a flicker of something unreadable crossing his weathered features. Defiance? Resignation?

The hesitant reply is a mere breath. "No." He pauses, his gaze sweeping over the worn mahogany of Rogers' desk, then locks back on the Governor. "But I do have one question."

Rogers leans forward, a predator poised. "Yes?"

"Will I be supplied with a ship? And a crew?" The question was simple: a desperate plea for something more than the scraps of a life already salvaged.

A slow, knowing smile, as chilling as a fog rolling in from the sea, spread across Rogers' face. "You have a ship, don't you, Captain Hornigold?" The implication is a lash, swift and sharp.

Hornigold's head shakes, a weary, almost dismissive gesture. The glint of the candlelight caught the silver in his beard. "Your crew," Rogers continues, his voice dropping to a conspiratorial whisper, "will be those that I select from the pirates that will be pardoned. Those whose necks are destined for the rope, now offered a different kind of dangling."

"With all due respect, Governor," Hornigold counters, his voice a low growl, the weariness replaced by a hardening resolve, "Do you truly believe these men will willingly carry out this task after being granted their lives? After tasting freedom?"

Rogers 'smile widens, revealing teeth that might once have gnashed in a fight. It's a smile that promises both salvation and damnation. "I don't think," he purrs, the sound like the sibilant hiss of a serpent, "they have much of a choice. Besides, as pardoned men on an errand for the British Royal Navy, they will be under the protection of England. A very comforting thought, wouldn't you agree, Captain?"

Hornigold takes a few calculated steps, the rough tapestry of his coat brushing against the back of the chair. He stands tall, a physical challenge to the man before him. "These men," he states, his voice resonating with the hard truth of his experience, "will be risking their lives."

Rogers turns to meet him, their faces now on the same level, the air between them thick with the unspoken understanding of men who have stared into the abyss. "You said it yourself, Captain," Rogers 'voice is a silken threat, "Risk. I believe those men down there," he gestures vaguely towards the unseen lower docks, "would infinitely rather risk their lives instead of ending them by the unforgiving snap of a hangman's noose."

Hornigold's fingers tightened around the brim of his hat, the worn leather cool beneath his touch. He meets Rogers 'unwavering gaze, a silent acknowledgement passing between them, a grim acceptance of the brutal bargain being struck. He nods. They sealed the pact, not with ink, but with the grim understanding of a shared, perilous future.

Queen Anne's Revenge

"If your last gnawing question has been ground to dust, Captain, the exit lies that way. See yourself out."

Hornigold's rough hands, calloused by rope and cutlass, settled his weathered tricorn back onto his salt-crusted scalp. A curt dip of the brim, a mocking salute.

He turned, the heavy oak door groaning a reluctant farewell as he pulled it open. A final, lingering look back at Rogers 'suffocatingly proper office. A torrent of unsaid truths surged, a volcanic whisper threatening to erupt, but a flicker of pragmatism, a deep, gnawing caution, choked it back. He turned again; the door slammed shut with the finality of a tomb.

Out of the stifling air of the fort, into the dusty, sunbaked sprawl of the town it guarded. Blair, a shadow etched against the bleached wood of the palisade, waited. As Hornigold emerged onto the thoroughfare, the familiar grit crunching underfoot,

Blair's voice cut through the lazy hum of the afternoon.

"Hornigold! What did the Governor's honeyed words yield?"

Catching up, his boots echoing the rhythm of Hornigold's, Blair's gaze was sharp, searching.

"The same poison I fed you before, Blair." Hornigold's voice was a low growl, a rumble of thunder promising a storm.

They walked, two wolves in tandem, the unspoken tension a palpable thing between them.

"He wants someone to hunt pirates?" Blair spat the words, a sneer twisting his lips. "Not someone. He wants me to carry out this devilish deed!"

Sweet Jesus, does he want me to grace this grand endeavor with my presence as well? Just the thought of betraying the code. He'd rather drown himself.

"That, my friend, depends entirely on whether his proclamation of pardon extends to you at the very moment it's publicly proclaimed." Hornigold's words were a careful dance, a veiled threat.

Blair's hands, calloused and strong, clamped onto Hornigold's shoulders, halting his stride. The sudden grip was a jolt, a desperate anchor.

"Well, for one, I am not afraid to sail into that particular storm." His voice was a challenge, a dare.

Hornigold let out a long, weary sigh, the sound like wind whistling through a broken mast. "I know you're not. But for the love of all that's holy, don't volunteer yourself for a venture that will probably get you killed."

Blair's gaze, unwavering, bore into Hornigold's. "And what of your friend, Blackbeard? What of him?" The question was heavy with unspoken history and a shared, dangerous camaraderie.

Hornigold's rough hand clamps down, a vice grip over Blair's mouth, stifling the breath, the very sound of protest. "Not a whisper," Hornigold's voice is a gravelly rasp against Blair's ear. "The Crown knows nothing. And they will know nothing. Going after the men Rogers wants is a betrayal enough for my own conscience. I feel like a renegade in my own skin."

Hornigold slowly and deliberately pulled his hand back, making Blair gasp as terror widened his eyes, which mirrored the gravity of the statement.

"If anyone dares to breathe the name 'Blackbeard,' or worse, 'Edward Teach,' you'll play the fool. Blank them. Empty-headed. Do you understand?"

Blair's head shakes, a frantic tremor. "I... I'm sorry, Ben. It's just... the lads. I'm worried for them all."

Hornigold's hand lands on Blair's shoulder, a heavy, perfunctory gesture. They resumed their pace, the rhythmic creak of the wood beneath their feet, punctuated by the distant, acknowledging nods of other pirates, their faces etched with suspicion and hard-won loyalty.

"We all are, mate," Hornigold murmurs, his gaze fixed on the horizon, a flicker of something unreadable–fear, perhaps, or grim resolve–in his eyes. "We all are."

The Queen Anne's Revenge and The Avenger cut through the turquoise waters off Rum Cay, their sails taut, like straining sinews against the salty spray. High above, lashed to the towering masts of the Revenge, Blackbeard's dread sigil, the grinning skeleton, snaps and writhes in the wind, a chilling promise. The decks thrum with the methodical rhythm of the crew–the snap of canvas, the scrape of swabs against weathered wood. Blackbeard, a towering figure against the endless expanse of sapphire sea, scans the horizon alongside his steersman, an unnerving stillness settling over the ship, a predator's calm before the strike. Rum Cay, a notorious haven for smugglers, its coastline a labyrinth of treacherous caves and submerged grottos, beckons with the scent of ill-gotten gains.

Blackbeard and his steersman pore over the shimmering water, their eyes, sharp and assessing, seeking the perfect mooring for their bounty. The helmsman points, his finger a decisive slash against the vibrant blue. "Captain. Ahead. That cove."

Blackbeard's head swivels, his gaze locking onto the shadowed indentation in the coastline. A predatory gleam entered his eyes. "Aye! Anchor us before that reef. I'll take a longboat, get a closer look." He turns, his voice booming across the deck, cutting through the salt-laced air like a harpoon. "Relay the order to The Avenger! Anchor off that point!"

A rough bellow from his bosun answers, "Aye, Captain!"

Blackbeard's gaze then falls upon Israel Hands, his face a mask of cold calculation. "Israel, pick yourself a man with shoulders like a bull. We're going to scout the perfect spot to begin this... transfer of goods."

The creak of timbers groaned a mournful symphony as Blackbeard, along with the gaunt Israel Hands and a nameless ruffian whose sweat already slicked his brow, crammed into the longboat. It was a crude cradle, a mere splinter of wood against the vast, indifferent canvas of the sea. A jarring lurch wrenched them from The Avenger's deck, and they plunged into the glassy, unnerving blue.

The air, thick with salt and the unspoken tension of anticipation, pressed in. As the longboat kissed the surface, a chilling ripple disturbed the placid facade. Blackbeard's hawk-like gaze, sharp enough to pierce the veil of any deception, swept over the side. Beneath the shimmering skin of the water, dark, predatory shapes glided, shadows with teeth. Sharks, circling like hungry specters. A guttural growl rumbled in his chest, a sound that promised violence.

He fixed his unnerving stare on Israel, a man whose eyes held the weary wisdom of a thousand betrayals, and the quivering crewman, whose fear was a palpable scent. "Don't even think of tumbling out, you fools!" His voice, a gravelly roar, scraped against the silence. "We've got company, the kind that doesn't wait for an invitation, swimming just below!"

Israel, his lean face a mask of hard-won cynicism, followed Blackbeard's gaze. The glint of predatory eyes beneath the surface sent a shiver, not of fear, but of grim recognition, through him. He met Blackbeard's glare, a sardonic twist to his lips. "Putting it mildly, Captain! That's a feast waiting to happen."

Below them, the colossal anchor of The Avenger plunged into the depths with a thunderous groan, a violent punctuation to their descent. The crewman, his knuckles white against the oars, began to churn the water into a frothy frenzy, desperation lending him unnatural strength.

"Row us into that crevasse," Blackbeard bellowed, pointing a gnarled finger towards a gaping, shadowed cavity in the cliff face, a dark promise of concealment.

As the oars bit deeper, a new movement disturbed the horizon. Across the treacherous coral, a second vessel materialized, a wraith slipping out of the mist, drawing perilously close to The Avenger. Israel's keen eyes, always scanning for threats, caught the subtle shift. He turned, his voice tight with urgency. "Captain! Another sail, rounding the point!"

Blackbeard snatched his spyglass, the polished brass cool against his calloused hand. His breath hitched, a predatory anticipation coiling in his gut. "A merchantman, perhaps?" he rasped, the question laced with a hunger for plunder. He raised the glass to his eye; the world shrank to a single, focused point. On the deck of The Avenger, a maelstrom of movement erupted. Men, mere specks from this distance, scurried like frantic ants, a prelude to the storm he knew was brewing.

Port Royal Calls

The salt spray stung Blackbeard's eyes as he spun around, the creak of the timbers a frantic counterpoint to his own thundering heart. Looming in the churning grey sea, a monstrous silhouette against the bruised sky–a British warship! The very air vibrated with menace. Then, a deafening roar ripped through the gale, a concussive blast from The Avenger's cannon ports, the acrid stench of gunpowder instantly fouling the briny air. Blackbeard's gaze snapped to the pale, sweat-slicked face of the rowing crewman, the man's eyes wide saucers reflecting the terror of the inferno.

"Blast it all, man! Back! BACK!" Blackbeard's voice, usually a guttural rumble that commanded obedience, was now a raw, desperate rasp, choked with the realization of their dire straits. "It's a leviathan of a warship... and it's spewing cannon fire at us!"

He could almost taste the rage, a bitter, metallic tang on his tongue. "They're hunting for easy coin, for rum-soaked scalawags!" he spat, the words a defiance against the encroaching dread. "But they've caught a tiger by the tail instead, haven't they?!"

Another cannon's thunderous bellow ripped through the air, closer this time, a jagged tear in the fabric of their fragile safety. A splinter of wood, hurled from the unseen fury, whipped past Blackbeard's ear with a wicked hiss. "Unbelievable!" he roared, the incredulity warring with a rising tide of cold fury. "By the depths, they dare attack us!"

The longboat, tossed like a child's toy on the heaving waves, finally slammed against The Revenge's barnacle-encrusted hull. Ropes snaked down, thick as pythons, their rough hemp biting into Blackbeard's calloused hands as he grasped them. The bosun's voice, a booming echo from above, vibrated through the very wood beneath them.

"We see it, Captain! We're raising the anchor!"

A frantic ballet of muscle and sinew erupted on deck. Men, their faces grim masks of determination, scrambled to hoist the heavy boat. The rhythmic thudding of their boots, the strained grunts of exertion, the groaning of the capstan–it all merged into a desperate symphony of survival. More cannons roared, each blast a hammer blow against their nerves.

"Hurry, you dogs! HURRY!" Blackbeard yelled, his voice raw, the desperation a palpable thing he felt seeping into his very bones.

The longboat lurched onto the deck, a chaotic tumble of limbs. Blackbeard, Israel–his trusted first mate, his shadow in this perilous game–and the terrified crewman spilled out, a whirlwind of motion and raw adrenaline.

Blackbeard launched himself across the splintered deck, the roar of the cannons a relentless drumbeat in his ears. Men were already a blur, their faces set, hoisting sails with a desperate urgency, their cutlasses glinting as they armed themselves, the steel singing its sharp, hungry song—Blackbeard's eyes, burning with a fierce, predatory light, fixed on the stern. There, the steersman wrestled the wheel, his knuckles white, his face a mask of frantic desperation, desperately wrestling the ship's massive helm, pivoting The Revenge towards the infernal fury of the warship. The air crackled with the unspoken threat; the coiled rage of a predator pushed to its breaking point.

"We're DOOMED! We'll never make it in time!" Israel, desperately clinging to the helm, turns the ship in frantic calculation.

"Half our plunder gone! Slipping through our grasp like sand!" Blackbeard slams his fist onto the deck.

Israel, his eyes blazing with a grim, unreadable fire, mirrors the fury. The steersman, a man carved from salt and desperation, wrestles the wheel with Israel, the wood groaning under the strain.

Blackbeard's gaze, fixed on its prey, locks onto Israel. A primal tension, thick and suffocating, vibrates between them.

"We're losing a ship! And a crew!" Blackbeard roars, his voice a thunderclap that drowns out the rising panic. "If we don't slam into them now, it's all over!"

The Revenge, a leviathan awakening, cuts through the churning waves, her speed a desperate, clawing ascent. They surge closer; the air crackling with impending violence. Blackbeard can taste the tang of gunpowder, see the fiery bloom of cannons erupting from both vessels. On the Avenger, his men are a defiant, desperate line, pistols spitting and blunderbusses roaring their defiance. The hulking British warship answers in kind, a leviathan of English oak and discipline, its soldiers a suffocating wave against the defiant few.

The air becomes a suffocating shroud, a choking nebula of smoke, the scent of burnt powder, and the raw, visceral screams of men. The Revenge breaches the inferno, drawing within spitting distance. Blackbeard's voice, a raw, primal roar, rips through the cacophony, aimed at the main deck:

"Are the cannons ready, damn you?" The bosun, his face a mask of grim resolve, his voice raspy with fear and defiance, bellows back, "Aye, Captain!" Blackbeard's voice, a thundering echo, orders, "FIRE!"

Fury Unleashed

The Revenge unleashed a singular, shattering roar of its cannon, a deafening prelude to its assault. The warship, already groaning under the onslaught, reeled. With a predatory grace, The Revenge surged, gliding along the port flank of The Avenger, its wounded hull a testament to the ferocity of the encounter. The air thrummed with a savage energy as Blackbeard's crew, a tide of unbridled ferocity, poured over the railings, their bodies a blur of motion. Crude planks, born of necessity, served as bridges, and the boarding party hurled them with brutal force. Grappling hooks, like talons of iron, clawed at the ravaged timbers of The Avenger, seeking purchase in the heart of the inferno.

As the vanguard of Blackbeard's relentless surge spilled onto the Amity, Captain Joseph Maynard, a figure forged in discipline and authority, descended the stern's ravaged staircase. His sword, a gleaming extension of his righteous fury, became a whirlwind of steel, cleaving and piercing through the encroaching horde. His gaze, a searing brand, locked onto the silhouette of Blackbeard, a dark god presiding over the chaos from The Avenger's railing.

Maynard fought his way through the maelstrom, a solitary lion against a pack of wolves, but the sheer, suffocating press of bodies, the guttural cries of combat, made progress a torment.

From the Amity's ravaged decks, British soldiers, their faces etched with grim determination, launched themselves onto ropes, attempting to bridge the blood-soaked chasm. Yet, they were met with a savage repulse, a tide of piratical fury that hurled them back. A volley of musket fire erupted, sharp cracks that tore through the din, sending men plummeting into the churning, brine-laced water that separated the two ships. From the shadowy depths below, a chorus of agonizing screams erupted. The reef's silent inhabitants, opportunistic predators, stirred. Sharks, sleek and ancient, surged through the blood-tinged currents, their obsidian eyes fixed on the struggling forms. Israel Hands, a coiled spring of desperation, snatched a loose rope, his intention a desperate bid for survival.

A searing agony ripped through Israel's shoulder. The world dissolved into a nauseating spin as he plummeted into the frigid, unforgiving embrace of the water between The Avenger and The Amity.

Blackbeard watched his first mate's descent, his hardened gaze unreadable as his man plunged into the crimson-stained water. A ragged, choked cry tore from Israel's throat. "Captain! Throw me a line! Captain!"

But the moment was a razor's edge, a breath held in the face of oblivion. "No time!" Blackbeard roared, his voice a thunderclap, and with a savage sweep of his cutlass, he severed a lifeline from The Avenger. He bellowed, his words a desperate plea against the roaring ocean. "Hold on!"

Blackbeard launched himself, a human projectile, arcing through the smoke-choked void between the two beleaguered ships. Cannons erupted, a percussive barrage, each deafening blast adding to the chaos as he swung through the inferno.

His hand, a gnarled anchor of strength, shot out, a desperate lifeline offered to the thrashing figure below, snatching Israel from the jaws of a monstrous shark poised to claim its prize. Blackbeard strained, his muscles screaming under the immense weight, his voice a raw, strained command to his first mate. "Grab hold of that cannon port!"

Israel, his senses reeling, lunged, his bloodied arm reaching for the shadowed opening. But his desperate grip snagged not the port, but the very cannon itself. A guttural scream of agony ripped from his lips as the searing metal bit into his flesh; his hold was tenuous, his body trembling with the effort. Blackbeard, with a Herculean surge, pulled himself towards the railing, his own grip a testament to his unwavering resolve.

From within the cannon port, a chorus of choked shouts, of men wrestling with burning flesh, echoed. Israel, his arms seared raw, screamed back. "Pull back that cannon so I can climb in!"

The very bones of both The Avenger and The Amity groaned, their timbers shrieking in protest as the relentless stress of the battle took its toll. They surrendered to the inevitable, a slow, agonizing descent into the hungry depths of the sea.

Blackbeard's gaze, a predator's glint, fixed upon the captain of The Amity. He seized another rope, a primal instinct driving him forward, and swung across the churning waters, landing not on the enemy deck, but directly into the bloody heart of the brawl.

With a guttural roar that ripped through the salt-laced air, Blackbeard drew his twin pistols, their steel glinting like malevolent stars. The thunder of their discharge shattered the chaos, each deafening crack spitting fire and lead into the dwindling ranks of soldiers. He moved with a predator's grace, a whirlwind of fury and powder smoke, his gaze locked on Maynard. The captain was locked in a desperate, brutal ballet with another rogue, their swords a blur of steel, a desperate clang echoing with each parry and thrust. Maynard's back, a beacon of vulnerability, was turned to the approaching storm.

Then, a final, desperate surge. Maynard's blade found its mark; a sickening crunch followed by the thud of a lifeless body hitting the blood-slicked deck. He turned, the victor for a fleeting, fatal second.

And there he was. Blackbeard. A monstrous silhouette against the inferno of battle, a pistol jammed against Maynard's forehead. Their eyes locked. In Maynard's, a primal terror bloomed, widening into two horrified orbs that reflected the infernal gleam in Blackbeard's own.

"Oh, God!" The whisper was torn from Maynard's throat, a plea swallowed by the deafening sounds of combat.

Blackbeard's gaze, cold as the abyss, held Maynard captive. "No," the pirate lord's voice rumbled, a low, chilling growl. "But you are about to meet him."

The shot. Not just a sound, but a physical force. A blinding flash, a searing pain, and then… oblivion. Maynard crumpled, a broken puppet, his life extinguished in a puff of decimating smoke. He fell, a husk, utterly lifeless.

The deck, a charnel house. Limbs tangled, a macabre mosaic of torn flesh and shattered bone, both pirate and soldier alike. And then, the inferno. Flames, hungry, clawed their way up the masts of The Amity, painting the night sky in shades of hellfire. The Avenger, too, groaned under the onslaught, both vessels succumbing to the embrace of the deep, sinking fast, a testament to the brutal dance of destruction.

Blackbeard stood amidst the wreckage, the embodiment of the storm's fury. From the churning, blood-tinged waters below, a symphony of terror rose–screams, sharp and piercing, as a writhing mass of tiger sharks, drawn by the scent of carnage, tore into the struggling soldiers, a testament to the savage, unforgiving nature of the sea.

Blackbeard's eyes, glinting in the smoke-choked air, raked over the carnage. The groaning timbers of his own ship were a symphony of defeat, yet a primal roar ripped from his throat, a raw command forged in the fires of desperation.

"Every soul still breathing! Back to the Revenge! A gut-wrenching bellow tore through the chaos, followed by a blinding flash. The Amity erupted, a monstrous bloom of fire and shrapnel. Then, a ravenous tongue of flame, an inferno unbound, lashed out, engulfing the sails of the Avenger in a furious embrace. With a violent shudder, the Revenge tore free, a wounded beast escaping the jaws of hell. As she limped away, a spectral silhouette against the dying light, Blackbeard and his shattered crew watched in stark, suffocating silence. The infernos raged, feeding on the sinking hulks, their dying groans swallowed by the sea.

At the Revenge's scarred stern, Israel, his arms a painful tapestry of burns, approached Blackbeard, his voice a raw rasp. "Captain? Have you ever witnessed such... madness?"

Blackbeard's gaze remained fixed on the burning pyre, his face a mask of stone. "Never."

Along the railing, a handful of men stood, their forms gaunt and skeletal against the vast ocean. Others lay sprawled on the deck, mere husks, their spirits as broken as their bodies. Israel, wincing with every movement, stood sentinel behind his captain. "Captain? We require a heading. A direction, lest we drift into oblivion."

A slow, deliberate turn. Blackbeard moved past Israel, the air around him thick with unspoken power. His voice, a low growl that promised retribution, cut through the residual din. "Get us out of here."

Later, as the Caribbean sky bled into a molten sunset, Israel stood outside the sanctum of Blackbeard's cabin. Behind him, the Revenge's crew, their faces etched with a profound weariness, a defeated stoicism, waited, their very souls yearning for an order, a purpose.

Israel's knuckles, raw and bruised, rapped against the weathered wood. A voice, deep and resonant, laced with an almost unnerving calm, drifted from within. "Enter!"

The door creaked open, revealing a scene bathed in the flickering amber glow of lamps. Israel stood at the threshold, a shadow in the dim light. Blackbeard, a monolith at the cabin's far end, stared out a rain-streaked window, his silhouette stark against the darkening sky.

He turned, his eyes still holding the embers of the inferno they had witnessed, met Israel's. A ghost of a smile, as sharp as a cutlass, played on his lips. "No need to linger in the doorway, Israel. Come in. Sit. Share this moment with me."

"Captain," Israel breathed, stepping further into the confines, the air heavy with the scent of aged rum and unspoken secrets.

Treacherous Passage

The heavy, salt-laced air in the cabin crackled with a tension as thick as the tar on the hull. Israel, a man etched with the grim realities of the sea, sank into the worn chair. The wood groaned a protest beneath him.

"I know why you're here, Israel," Blackbeard's voice, a low rumble like distant thunder, sliced through the silence. "The men... they're trembling, aren't they? Like newborn lambs to the slaughter."

Israel's gaze, a storm cloud in human form, flickered from the scarred surface of the table to the formidable silhouette of Blackbeard. He let out a breath that tasted of brine and defeat. "Of course, they are. Who wouldn't be?"

"I can't make sense of it, Israel. Not a lick," Blackbeard admitted, his broad chest heaving. "This... this unraveling... it blinds me as much as it blinds you."

"Did we... did we somehow swallow a viper in Tortuga?" Israel's voice was rough, a rasp against the raw wound of their misfortune. "A spy?"

"Possible. Damned possible. My eyes saw nothing, felt nothing. Did yours?" Blackbeard's eyes, dark and probing, bored into Israel.

"No," Israel stated, the word a heavy stone dropped into the well of their uncertainty.

"How? How could this happen?" The words tore from Blackbeard's throat, a raw, guttural cry. "We are better than this! We are the serpent's own teeth, not its fallen scales!"

A tremor ran through Israel's frame. "So much... so much is gone, Edward."

Blackbeard slammed a fist onto the table, the wood shuddering. The sudden, violent sound made Israel flinch, a phantom ache blooming in his own fists. "Yes! So much IS gone! The very lifeblood of our endeavors, bled dry!"

Israel's chair scraped back with a shriek that echoed the anguish in his soul. He rose, his shadow stretching long and gaunt across the planks. "The crew... they would follow you into the depths of hell itself, Edward. But they need to know. They need to know if what was lost can ever be clawed back from the depths. These waters... they are no longer a sanctuary. They are a butcher's block."

Blackbeard, his back to Israel, stared out the salt-streaked window, his profile a study in grim resolve.

The setting sun bled a sickly orange across the horizon. "The King's hounds," he spat, the words laced with venom. "They sniff the air. They're finally making a concerted effort to scour the Caribbean clean of us. To erase us."

He turned, his eyes meeting Israel's with a fire that refused to be extinguished. "But I have a plan, Israel. A desperate, glorious plan. It is the very destination we sought after securing our plunder."

"Where?" The question was a desperate plea, a whispered prayer in the face of uncertainty.

"You'll know soon enough," Blackbeard's voice was a dark promise. He moved towards the door, his imposing form filling the frame. Then, he paused, his gaze locking onto Israel once more, a chilling intensity in their depths. "Do you still trust me, Israel? Even now, with the taste of defeat so strong in our mouths?"

Israel's gaze was unwavering, a mirror reflecting the raw, untamed spirit of the man before him. "We've spilled blood before, Edward. We've danced with death hand in hand. I would be a fool to doubt you now."

Blackbeard's jaw tightened, a flicker of something–relief, perhaps, or a rekindled fury–passing across his weathered face. Failure was a concept he did not entertain. It was a foreign language, a beast he could never graze in the pastures of his mind. Regardless of the odds, regardless of the cost, the thought of himself being defeated was an impossibility. It simply was not on the map of his existence.

The creak of the weathered planks beneath their boots was a mournful symphony as Blackbeard and Israel emerged onto the salt-laced deck. A hush, heavy as a shroud, fell over the crew. Eyes, raw and red-rimmed, flickered upwards, a desperate plea glinting in their depths. The air, thick with the stench of stale sweat and drying blood, pressed down, a physical manifestation of their despair. The deck, a tapestry of torn canvas and splintered wood, bore witness to the brutal ballet of battle, and the men's faces showed a brutal harvest of wounds. As Blackbeard's piercing gaze swept across the huddled mass, a cold, sharp dread settled in his gut–morale hadn't just dipped; it had plunged into the abyss.

"You men," his voice, a gravelly rumble honed by a thousand storms, cut through the silence, "look as if the very hand of Death has been clawing at your souls."

From the shadow of a rigging, a figure detached himself, the Bosun's Mate, his frame gaunt, his gaze fixed and hollow. "And that's how we feel, Cap'n," he rasped, his voice like sandpaper on bone. "We've lost... nearly everything."

Blackbeard's gaze, as sharp as a cutlass, found a lone figure slumped on an overturned crate, his shoulders hunched as if bearing the weight of the world.

Trade Routes Call

"You! Drag the rest of them up like the dead they nearly are!"

Blackbeard, a storm brewing in his own eyes, loomed at the stern of The Revenge. The deck, a canvas of creaking timbers and snapping canvas, breathed a chilling stillness. The only symphony is the rasp of the waves against the hull, the mournful keening of the wind through the rigging, and the taut, anxious snapping of ropes. A knot of men, their faces etched with weariness and a grim, unvoiced fear, assembled, all eyes–a desperate, hungry constellation fixed on their captain.

"I see the exhaustion clawing at you. I taste the longing for solid ground, for lives unburdened by the brine and blood. I know many of you crave escape." His voice, a gravelly rasp like stones grinding together, cut through the quiet. "I say, no. This life… it's a war fought with every sunrise. And you men, you've shown me your teeth today, twice over. There is no doubt in my mind. If you yearn for oblivion, for the soft embrace of anonymity, then go. No man among you will bear my scorn for it."

He pauses, letting the unspoken truth hang heavy in the salty air. "But if you want to reclaim what this cursed day attempted to rip from your hands and seize back the future you believed was lost... then follow me.

His gaze swept across them, sharp and piercing. "Imagine intercepting those plump, unsuspecting merchants. Imagine their cargo, ours. Imagine the profit, not plucked from the jaws of death, but earned."

A figure, the Bosun, knuckles whitening as he grips his forearms, breaks from the huddled mass. His voice, though rough, trembles with a desperate pragmatism. "Captain, what if no one will deal with us?"

Blackbeard's lips curl into a predatory grin, a flash of something ancient and dangerous in his eyes. "They will. And you know why they will? Because they will be free. Free from the greedy claws of England's taxes! That's why. Stay with me, just one more year. One more orbit of this unforgiving world, and I will carve that truth into your very souls. What say you, men?"

The crew exchanged glances, a silent debate raging behind their tired eyes. Then, with a sound that echoes the very core of their being, Blackbeard's cutlass bares its steel, glinting like a sliver of captured moonlight. "What say you?" A guttural roar erupts, a wave of desperate assent that washes over the deck, a collective defiance against the fading light.

"And if we must carve our passage through a few damned English souls to claim it, then so be it!" Blackbeard's speech was not just a plan; it was a promise. Money moved men. And when you can guarantee it, no man worth his salt will dare turn it down.

The air in the courtyard hung thick and heavy, a suffocating blanket woven from salt spray, unwashed bodies, and the taste of fear. British soldiers, a grim, silent wall of scarlet, bristled along the fort's battlements, their muskets glinting brightly under the harsh Caribbean sun. Below them, in the churning sea of the courtyard, a throng of hardened faces–pirates, every one–shifted impatiently, their arms crossed like shields against the unseen currents of fate. They were a tinderbox, awaiting a spark from Governor Rogers, who now ascended to a raised platform, a solitary, imposing figure against the blinding sky. The scent of stale rum and desperate hope mingled with the dry rustle of parchment as notaries, poised at scarred wooden tables, readied their quills.

Rogers, a man whose voice was as sharp as a cutlass edge, stepped forward, hands clasped behind his back in a pose of chilling control. The expectant hush was so profound it felt like a physical pressure, a dam about to break.

"Good day, gentlemen," his voice boomed, echoing off the stone walls, each syllable a hammer blow. "We shall not keep you long. For you are among the first to claim England's generous gift–a contract that shall erase your past." A ripple of murmurs, a mixture of relief and suspicion, snaked through the crowd. "However," he continued, his gaze sweeping over the anxious faces, "the Crown will ask some of you to undertake a small errand."

Beside one another, Hornigold and Blair exchanged a look, a silent acknowledgment of the tightrope they walked. Blair, his scarred cheek twitching, leaned in, a sardonic whisper escaping his lips like a serpent's hiss. "He means for him." A flicker of amusement, quick and dangerous, crossed Hornigold's face. He silenced Blair with a sharp, almost imperceptible gesture, his finger pressed to his lips.

"I require lines," Rogers declared, his voice hardening. "Each of you will state your name, and then make your mark, witnessed by these esteemed gentlemen." He paused, letting his gaze linger on Hornigold, a predator singling out its prey. "Since you have seen fit to appoint Benjamin Hornigold to speak for this collection of individuals..."

Hornigold muttered under his breath, a guttural rumble barely audible above the throng. "Here it comes."

"...I have tasked him," Rogers finished, his voice laced with a dark amusement, "with leading a crew to hunt down two particular scoundrels who have been plaguing New Providence." A collective intake of breath. "Those among you who volunteer for this endeavor will be granted special privileges. Privileges that will pave the way for a truly new life, with considerably less difficulty." He gestured towards the notaries. "If you wish to volunteer, do so discreetly with the gentlemen at the tables. That is all." With a final, piercing look, Rogers retreated, melting back into the shadows of the soldiers.

A cacophony of shouts erupted as the soldiers, their boots thudding like war drums, carved paths through the pirate ranks, herding them towards the tables. Blair, his gaze locked on Hornigold as they were swept into the nascent line, spoke, his voice laced with genuine curiosity. "Do you think many will step forward?"

Hornigold's eyes, dark and shadowed, met Blair's. A bitter smile touched his lips. "I know not. But it is kind of the Governor to so publicly announce that I am the leader of this betrayal."

As they shuffled forward, the raw scent of fear, thick and cloying, seemed to deepen. "You're truly dreading this, aren't you?" Blair's voice was softer now, a thread of unexpected concern.

Hornigold's response was a raw whisper, a confession torn from the depths of his soul. "With every fiber of my being."

He reached a notary table, the worn wood smooth beneath his trembling hand. The ink on the parchment, black as pitch, beckoned. He began to sign, the scratch of his quill a stark, lonely sound in the sudden, profound silence.

Edward Teach

The air vibrated with the raw, guttural impatience of a caged beast. Pirates, a sea of weathered faces etched with a thirst for violence and gold, crammed into lines that snaked towards the fort's entrance. Their eyes darted from the imposing stone walls above to the distant horizon, each man a coiled spring of barely contained fury. Hundreds more, a restless tide of island dwellers and freshly arrived brigands, massed beyond the ramparts, a hungry, feral pack awaiting their entry. Redcoats, their disciplined ranks a stark contrast to the chaotic throng below, patrolled the ramparts themselves, their gaze sharp and watchful, like hawks circling their prey.

Across the shimmering expanse of the bay, the docks seethed with furious energy. The water teemed with a monstrous ballet of ships–behemoths docking with groaning timbers and swift sloops darting out like predatory fish. The Union Jack, a defiant splash of crimson against the azure sky, snapped with arrogant authority from atop the fort and every mast, a stark declaration of England's iron grip on New Providence.

Aboard the bustling docks, amidst the cacophony of hammers and shouted orders, Hornigold and Blair materialized from the throng. Their presence, a palpable force of dangerous charisma, cut through the grime and sweat of honest labor. The rhythmic clatter of hooves announced a different arrival. A polished carriage, a symbol of the civilized world incongruously thrust into this lawless den, rumbled to a halt. Governor Rogers surveyed the scene from within, flanked by two hawk-eyed soldiers on horseback, their polished steel glinting in the harsh sun.

Hornigold, his gaze like a hawk, turned to meet Rogers' ascent. "Good morning, Captain."

A curt nod from Hornigold. "Morning."

"I trust the men I've selected will serve you well." Hornigold's lips curved into a smile that promised more than it revealed, a flicker of amusement playing in his eyes. "That depends," he drawled, the words laced with a subtle mockery, "if we can get all of them together."

Rogers, ensconced in the velvet interior of the carriage, his gaze piercingly direct, looked down at the pirate captain. "Do you feel you are being treated unfairly, Captain?"

Hornigold's grin widened, a sharp, dangerous thing. "I'm not subject to say what's unfair, sir."

Rogers leaned back, a subtle shift that spoke volumes. A palpable wave of silent aggravation, thick as sea mist, washed over him. "Well," he conceded, his voice a low rumble, "it beats the alternative, doesn't it, Captain Hornigold?" The unspoken threat hung in the air, as heavy and suffocating as the tropical humidity.

Hornigold's head snaps up, a grimace twisting his features. "Aye. Just don't expect me to stomach what I have to do. Sir." The unspoken weight of his words, a promise of reluctant duty laced with bitter resentment.

Rogers, his gaze sharp as a shard of glass, offered a curt nod. "Agreed. I've no doubt the seas teem with far fouler creatures than I've had the misfortune to name, Captain." The hint of the sinister in his voice, a subtle acknowledgment of shared darkness, did not escape Hornigold.

A harsh, barked laugh ripped from Hornigold's throat, echoing the caws of the carrion birds circling overhead. "Aye, Governor! That be true." The sound was raw, a defiance hurled against the suffocating certainty of the gallows 'shadow.

Rogers 'lips curved into a smile that didn't reach his eyes, a chillingly controlled expression as he gestured to the waiting carriage. "Consider it this way, Captain. You still draw breath. Some of us," he let the implication hang, sharp and pointed, "are not so fortunate."

Hornigold spun around, his eyes locking onto Blair, who was meticulously, almost cruelly, reciting the names of the condemned. The rustle of parchment, the drone of Blair's voice–it all seemed to amplify the thrum of dread in the air. Hornigold's boots crunched on the coarse gravel as he strode towards Blair, his shadow elongating, a certain stealth in his stride.

"What a craven cur!" The words were spat, laced with a venom that could curdle milk. "He should be up there, rotting. Not these men." Blair's arm shot out, his finger jabbing towards the nearby gallows. The sight was a tableau of grim finality: the swaying forms of hanged pirates, their flesh already yielding to the gnawing beaks of crows, their vacant eyes staring at a sky that offered no solace. The stench of decay, a sickly sweet perfume, rose to meet them.

"I second that!" The words ripped from Hornigold's throat, raw and jagged. Sweat, thick and cloying, slicked his brow, a testament to the heat, or perhaps something far more primal, that warred within him.

He swiped at it, the rough fabric of his sleeve a coarse whisper against his skin. "Hard to believe that man," he rasped, his gaze snagging on Blair, "was ever a pirate."

Ten years. A lifetime. Enough time to scour the gleam from a man's eyes, to etch lines of sin and survival onto his very soul. Enough time to transform a swaggering rogue into a hardened husk. "Ten years can carve a man into a different beast entirely."

Hornigold's eyes narrowed. "But you… you haven't changed, Blair. Not in ten years." The observation was accurate.

Blair's hand, gnarled and calloused, traced the contours of his own face, a phantom touch against skin that remembered different wars. "A bit more gray," he admitted, his voice a low rumble, like distant thunder. "And… not quite as quick."

A guttural bark, more beast than human, erupted from Hornigold. "Quick?" he scoffed, the word laced with a truth that made the hairs on Blair's neck prickle. "You were never quick, Blair. You were always something… else. A good man, yes. But quick? That's a memory that never took root." His laughter echoed, a chilling reminder of the dark paths they had both, in their own ways, walked.

The Man. The Legend.

The Revenge has sailed its way across the vast, churning Atlantic, its hungry prow now aimed at the North Carolina coast. The salty tang of the sea, laced with the rank, sweet scent of spilled grog, hung heavy in the air. On deck, a tableau of rough men, their faces etched with sun and storm, found a moment's respite. The clatter of pewter mugs, the inaudible murmur of guttural laughter, and the rasp of voices fueled by potent spirits formed a restless symphony.

Then, a shadow fell. Jack Roberts, a lad barely out of boyhood, his youthful skin still bearing the flush of the sun, approached Israel. The rough weave of his worn shirt brushed against the older sailor's arm as he dared to tap his shoulder.

Israel turned. His eyes, dark and sharp, raked over Roberts. The boy was a flicker against the backdrop of seasoned brutality.

"Yes, boy," Israel's voice, a low rumble like distant thunder, vibrated with a mixture of weariness and a keen, unsettling amusement.

"I... I wanted to ask about the Captain." Roberts' voice, though trying for boldness, held a tremor that betrayed his unease.

Israel's arms, thick as seasoned oak, crossed over his chest. The simple gesture seemed to anchor him. A man rooted in the primal earth of the sea. "What do you want to know?"

"I've been talking," Roberts confessed, his gaze darting to the stern, where a figure commanded the very air around him. "With the men. No one... no one seems to know much about him. So I thought I'd ask you."

A slow, knowing smirk spread across Israel's weathered face, a landscape of scars and unspoken stories. "Well, I'll tell you, boy. He's a rare man. A true pirate." His words were a pronouncement, a decree.

Both men's gazes, drawn by an invisible force, ascended to the stern. There, a colossus of a man, cloaked in darkness and festooned with the terrifying glint of weaponry, stood sentinel. Blackbeard, his beard a black, flowing tide, held aloft a bottle of rum, its amber contents catching the dying light like a captured sunset. The very air crackled with his presence, a palpable force that both intimidated and mesmerized.

"He has thirteen wives," Israel continued, his voice dropping to a near whisper, as if imparting secrets stolen from the wind. "Caches of riches that even we... we don't know of. But know this, above all, boy." He leaned closer, his breath, hot and pungent with grog, ghosting Roberts' ear. "If you follow him, he'll make sure you'll never fall in a fight. You'll be as unyielding as the ocean floor."

Roberts swallowed, his Adam's apple bobbing like a buoy in choppy seas. The sheer weight of Israel's words, the raw power they hinted at, left him breathless, a moth caught in the orbit of a consuming flame. He nodded, his young mind reeling, trying to grasp the immensity of the man who commanded such awe.

"Remember," Israel's finger, thick and calloused, rose to his lips, a silent vow. He lowered it, the gesture a final, intimate seal on their exchange. "Not a word, boy." Then, a flicker of something akin to mischief danced in his dark eyes. "I forgot to mention," he added, his voice regaining its jovial, yet menacing, tone. "He loves to tell stories."

With a bellow that seemed to shake the very timbers of the Revenge, Israel called out, "Captain! Will you be so kind as to entertain us with a story?"

Blackbeard's head swiveled, his eyes, burning coals in the encroaching twilight, fixed on Israel. A low, rumbling laugh, like stones grinding against each other, emanated from him. "A story, Israel?"

"Aye!" the crew erupted in a surge of anticipation, their earlier weariness vanishing like mist before the sun.

Blackbeard, the very embodiment of dread, descended the stairs, the bottle of rum a scepter in his grasp. His voice, when it boomed, was a tempest, a force of nature unleashed. "Gather 'round, men! I have a story! A story I have!" He raised the bottle, his shadow stretching long and distorted. "I kill whom I choose, when I choose! I slay when offended! I slay sometimes for pleasure when I'm not at all offended! Why?" He paused, letting the silence hang heavy, pregnant with unspoken threat. "For you!"

The men roared their approval, a primal cheer echoing across the waves. "More!" they bayed.

"Once," Blackbeard rasped, his voice laced with a chilling glee, "I took a Dutch captain's ship! Instead of killing him, I cut off his lips! I cut off his ears and shaved off his nose! I shot him in his bowels when he would not eat those!"

A wave of savage laughter, a guttural outpouring of dark amusement, washed over the deck. The scent of fear, now mingled with a perverse exhilaration, filled the air.

"I reward those who follow me," Blackbeard roared, his voice a thunderclap, "and I kill those who oppose me! I bring Hell with me, there is no doubt! But if you want a moral to this tale," he lowered his voice, a sinister intimacy creeping in, "I only have one to tout! There's a devil in all of us, there's no doubt! But is he trying to get in us, or is he trying to get out?" The question hung in the salt-laced air, a chilling echo of the darkness that lived not just in Blackbeard, but in the hearts of every man who followed him.

The din of triumphant roars hammered Roberts ' ears, a primal surge of guttural exclamations punctuated by the clatter and scrape of raised tankards. He spun towards Israel, his breath catching, a raw, animalistic shock seizing him. Did he truly do that?

Israel's gaze met his, a fiery glint dancing in their depths, a slow, unsettling smile stretching across their lips. The question remained, thick with unspoken menace. "What? Shoot a man in the bowels?" A low chuckle, like gravel grinding, rumbled in Israel's chest.

"Aye," Roberts spat, his own voice a rasp, "among the other transgressions."

Israel's smirk widened, a chilling testament to their history. "I've witnessed far graver deeds."

An icy dread, sharp as a splinter of ice, pierced Roberts. "Sweet Jesus!" The words were ripped from his throat, raw and ragged. He backed away, the rough planks of the deck grating beneath his boots, each step a desperate retreat from the abyss Israel represented.

As he moved, a hulking shadow fell over him. Blackbeard brushed past, his calloused hand landing with a thud on Roberts 'shoulder, a gesture that felt both congratulatory and deeply unsettling. Roberts froze, a jolt of primal fear shooting through him. He twisted, his eyes locking onto Blackbeard's, a silent, desperate plea for understanding. But Blackbeard offered none; his gaze unwavering, as he moved to stand before Israel.

"Another soul yearns for the whisper of my legend?" Blackbeard's voice was a deep, resonant growl, the sound vibrating through the ship's very timbers.

Israel raised their tankard, the amber liquid catching the flickering lantern light, a silent toast. "Naturally. They all thirst for tales of 'Blackbeard'." The name was spoken with a reverence that bordered on blasphemy.

"And what truths did you impart?" Blackbeard pressed, his eyes narrowed, a dangerous curiosity igniting within them.

Israel's laugh was a dry, crackling sound, like burning parchment. "Just enough," they purred, their gaze returning to Roberts, a chilling triumph in their eyes, "to leave him in a state of utter, soul-shattering bewilderment."

"Keep this up, Israel, and you'll have me staring at an empty deck. They'll be so frayed, so torn, they won't know if they're meant to sail under my flag or leap into the abyss."

Israel, a shadow in the lamplight, chuckled, the sound like gravel grinding. He raised a bottle to his lips, the amber liquid catching the firelight. "If they jump, Blackbeard, at least they'll carry the raw terror of your name to their graves!" He tilted the bottle, a long, slow draught, his eyes never leaving the captain.

"It's a damn miracle, ain't it?" Blackbeard's voice was a low rumble, laced with a savage satisfaction. "How much legend a man can forge in such a short period of time."

"And what's it like, Captain," Israel purred, the question a serpent's hiss, "to know that your very shadow precedes you? That your face is a brand burned into the world's memory?"

Blackbeard's chest expanded, a deep breath, and a strong exhale. "It's a power, Israel. A raw, gut-churning thing you can't begin to comprehend. To stride through a throng and feel the air thicken with dread. To lock eyes with a stranger and watch their very soul shrink, their gaze splintering away like shattered glass."

A heavy stillness descended, thick with unspoken menace. Then, Blackbeard's gaze, sharp as a cutlass, snagged on the edge of the world. A single, insistent pulse of light. It blinked. And blinked again. A sequence, etched into his very bones. Recognition, cold and sharp, pierced through him.

"Israel," his voice dropped, a predator's growl. "That flicker. Do you see it?"

Israel tilted his head, the shadow of his brow deepening. "Aye, Captain. Is that...?"

"...It is." Blackbeard's knuckles whitened on the railing. "To the stern, Israel. Now. Repeat that sequence!"

He watched, a smile playing on his lips, as the vessel drew nearer, its silhouette sharpening against the star-dusted canvas. "This... this new turn in our voyage," Blackbeard breathed, the scent of salt and destiny on the wind, "this will birth empires."

New World

The White Cloud, a behemoth of Spanish oak, scraped alongside the Queen Anne's Revenge, a guttural groan of timber against timber that vibrated through the brine-laced air. On her impossibly high rail, a phalanx of pirates, weathered faces grim and eyes like chips of flint, leaned out, a gleaming gaze fixed upon Blackbeard's infamous vessel. Then, a ripple of movement from the ship's shadows – a presence emerged, silhouetted against the lamplight. Morgan LaFaye. Tall as a mast, with a beauty as sharp and dangerous as a cutlass's edge, she materialized, her voice a low, silken challenge that sliced through the creak of the rigging.

"Is that the devil himself I see lurking in the mist?"

A raw, animalistic bark tore from Blackbeard's throat. With a vice-like grip on a fraying length of rope, he hauled his formidable frame onto the very lip of his own railing, his legion of cutthroats massed behind him, a menacing tide of scarred flesh and glinting steel. The salty spray kissed his beard, a wild mane whipped by the wind, and his eyes, twin coals burning with an unholy fire, locked onto Morgan.

"A sight to behold, Morgan. Your ship... a queen in her own right." His voice rumbled, a dangerous purr that promised both pleasure and peril.

The air thickened as Morgan's men, with practiced brutality, began to fling ropes, thick as a serpent's coil, towards the Revenge. The savage laughter of Blackbeard's crew answered, their hands blurring as they began to haul the colossal galleon in, the timbers groaning under the strain like a wounded beast.

"Why don't you grace me with a proper welcome, Captain?" Morgan's voice, now laced with an almost audible hunger, echoed across the gap. "Come, share my deck."

With a sudden, violent tug, Blackbeard ripped a mooring line free. He moved with an unnatural grace, a dark image descending, and glided across the turbulent water towards Morgan's ship. Israel, his own brute force etched into every line of his face, turned to the men securing the lines, his voice a gravelly roar that barely carried over the wind.

"Hold fast, you curs! Let not a single fathom slacken!"

Blackbeard landed on the deck not with a thud, but with the stillness of a striking snake, directly before

Morgan. The scent of gunpowder and sweat, mingled with the sharp tang of the sea, clung to him.

"It is... good to see you again." Blackbeard's eyes, dark pools reflecting the storm gathering within him, raked over Morgan's form. A slow smile, a flash of white against his sun-darkened face, spread across his lips. "How long has it been? Has the sea devoured two full years since last we met?"

Morgan's gaze, equally piercing, met his, a silent acknowledgment of a history as turbulent and unforgiving as the waters that separated them. "At least that, Edward. At least that."

From the depths of his tattered coat, Blackbeard produced an onion bottle, its dark, viscous contents sloshing with a promise of a good night. A guttural chuckle rumbled in his chest, a sound like stones grinding together. "I have a bottle."

A sultry gleam ignited in Morgan's eyes, mirroring the flicker of the lantern. With a snap that echoed the readiness of a viper, she produced her own, a slim, dark vessel that felt ancient in her grasp. "And I have mine!" Her voice, a low purr laced with challenge, "Want to go below and see who finishes first?"

Blackbeard's smile was a jagged tear through the shadow of his legendary beard, a promise of both danger and dark delight. The scent of brine and old rum, clinging to him like a second skin, intensified. "After you, Captain."

Within the oppressive intimacy of the Captain's Quarters aboard The White Cloud, Morgan's teeth, sharp and surprisingly elegant, tore at the cork. The pop was a defiant burst, followed by the fiery assault of rum as it scorched its way down her throat, a liquid ember chasing away the chill of the night air. She exhaled, a wisp of vapor carrying the sharp tang of liquor.

"I've heard whispers," she began, her voice now a silken thread weaving through the tension, "that the King's hounds are sniffing your trail. Is that why you've sailed these desolate waters, Edward?" The question is heavy with unspoken history and veiled accusations.

Blackbeard's gaze, eyes glowing from lamp light, met hers. "You heard that, did you?" A hint of amusement, cold and sharp, touched his lips.

He moved then, not with haste, but with the deliberate power of a coiled serpent. The heavy oak chair scraped against the deck with a violent shriek, a prelude to the unspoken contest that had begun. He settled before her, his presence a palpable force that filled the small room. The smell of sweat, sea salt, and something wild and untamed emanated from him. "What are you up to, Edward?" Morgan's question was softer now, a siren's call, the challenge momentarily replaced by a flicker of genuine, unsettling curiosity.

Blackbeard's gaze, a tempest in his stormy dark eyes, snapped upwards. Annoyance, sharp and raw, coiled in his gut.

"I don't go by that name anymore." His voice, a gravelly rumble that had weathered a thousand gales, vibrated with barely suppressed fury. "You truly don't expect me to call you Blackbeard? Never!"

He gestured wildly, a hand scarred by salt and shot, towards the darkening horizon. "The Crown tightens its grip, its icy fingers crawling across the Caribbean. We fled north to the Carolinas! To carve out new empires, to seize the very arteries of trade!"

Morgan's voice sliced through his fervor, a siren's call laced with danger. "The trade routes, Edward? What forbidden knowledge burns in your skull that I do not possess?"

A flicker, something ancient and untamed, ignited in Blackbeard's eyes. "My secrets are my own, my love. And I shall guard them with my life!"

Morgan's stare was a predator's; her one raised eyebrow a silent challenge. The scent of brine and something musky, undeniably feminine, wafted from her. "And what are you waiting for? Come. Claim what is yours!"

He downed a fiery swallow of rum, the burn a welcome distraction from the fire she stoked within him. "You are a tempest, a she-devil clad in silk and fury." He moved, drawn by an irresistible force, the worn leather of his boots creaking against the deck.

"But tonight," she whispered, her voice thick with anticipation, "I am your devil."

Morgan's touch was electric, igniting his very soul. She pulled him close, the clash of their bodies a prelude to the storm. Their kiss was a desperate, devouring thing, a primal need unleashed. The rough canvas of his vest tore under her urgent fingers, each rip a surrender, a shedding of defenses.

She lay atop him, a vision of dark beauty, her raven hair a silken curtain against his sweat-slicked skin. The air crackled with their shared exertion, the humid night pressing in on their unleashed passion.

"No man," she breathed, her voice a husky whisper against his ear, "has ever made me feel this... alive."

Blackbeard's smile was a dangerous curve of his lips, a hint of the madness that defined him. "Why do you torment me so?"

Morgan pulled back, her eyes glittering with amusement and something far more profound. "Torment? I would hardly call this pleasure 'torment'."

"It is," he insisted, his voice rough with a yearning that ached deep within his bones. "Because you will never truly be mine."

Morgan's laughter, a wild, intoxicating sound, echoed in the darkness. "But I just was."

"You know what I mean," he pleaded, his usual swagger dissolving into raw vulnerability. "Marry me."

Her smile widened, a slow, captivating unveiling. The distant crash of waves seemed to echo the tumultuous beating of his heart.

Two Ships Pass in the Night

"Never enough," she breathed, her voice a silken rasp against the coarse tangle of his beard. "Don't you drown in your wives, Edward? Are they not a sea to spill into?"

He felt the phantom tickle of her fingers weaving through the wiry forest of his chin, a scent of sea salt and something dangerously sweet clinging to her skin. "Every one of them, a paltry droplet. I'd trade them all for one drop of you."

"Another life," she whispered, the words a chill breath against his ear, a promise and a curse.

He felt her shift, the yielding weight of her body a sudden absence against his. He sat up, the rough canvas of his breeches a stark contrast to the memory of her skin. "What vexes you, Edward? Is it a storm brewing within you? Are you not content?"

"Content?" His laughter was a brittle shard. "We've festered in this damned cabin long enough. Another dawn and your men won't respect you." He heard the rustle of his linen, the rasp of leather as he armed himself. "Edward... wait!" The desperation in her cry snagged at him, a sharp hook pulling at his gut. He turned, the glint of the lamp catching the fierce intelligence in her eyes, the vulnerable plea beneath the defiance. "Yes?"

"Be… careful. Out there." Her voice cracked, a raw vulnerability that belied the steely resolve he usually saw.

A slow smile, as deep as the sea itself, stretched across his lips. He saw her again, not the woman who shivered in his arms, but the woman he could never have. "Do you truly not know me, woman? I am the storm."

Morgan's gaze, sharp as a cutlass, rakes over Blackbeard. "Is this truly how you intend to depart?"

A pregnant pause stretches between them, heavy with unspoken history. Blackbeard's eyes, dark pools reflecting the flickering lamplight, fix on her for a beat too long before his fingers, calloused and scarred, slide the worn leather of his baldric into place. The rasp of the leather against his weathered tunic is a low growl.

"Remember our last encounter, my dear Morgan," he said, his voice a rumble like distant thunder, laced with a dangerous weariness. "You called us 'two ships that pass in the night.' And so we are. So we shall eternally remain." Each word is a hammer blow, forging a truth both stark and immutable.

He turns, his broad back a silhouette against the dim cabin light, and strides towards the door. His boots thudded on the wooden floor, a final, measured rhythm. At the threshold, he paused, his head cocked, and cast one last look at Morgan. The silence that descends is not empty, but thrumming with the unexpressed, the unspoken yearning and the bitter resignation. Then, with a decisive click of the latch, the door swung open, and he was gone.

Across the vast, heaving expanse of the Atlantic, where the Caribbean sun beats down with fiery intensity, Hornigold stands sentinel. The salt spray kissed his weathered cheeks, the briny scent clinging to his rough spun shirt. He is the undeniable core of this gathered force, rooted beside the ship's proud mainmast. The assembled crew, a motley collection of hardened men, pressed in around him, their faces etched with a potent blend of anticipation and simmering impatience. The air crackled with their unspoken questions.

With a deliberate, almost ritualistic movement, Hornigold selects a sharp piece of metal. The scraping sound as he carves into the stout wood of the mast echoes with a primal resonance.

"September 18th, 1717," he pronounces, his voice a whip crack that cuts through the murmuring crowd.

"Men, remember this act!" he commanded, his eyes blazing with fierce conviction. "This date, carved into this mast, will not simply mark time. It will herald a new dawn for this very vessel, a chapter yet unwritten in its brutal history."

He turns then, his gaze sweeping over the faces closest to him, a hunter surveying his pack. The raw power emanating from him is palpable, a force that seems to bend the very wind to his will. "I have been tasked," he continues, the words a low growl that stirs a tremor of unease, "to lead you. To hunt down our brethren. Men, you all know." He pauses, letting the implication hang heavy in the humid air. "As of this very moment, we stand on the precipice of betrayal. We are about to tear asunder the very covenant we swore, the sacred oath that bound us."

A gruff voice, raspy with years of shouting orders and curses, erupts from the throng. "Betrayal?" And the world, for these men, teeters on the brink of a precipice.

Bath Town

"So, what's the play, then?" A rough voice rasped, cutting through the salty air like a splinter of wood. "Aren't we all pardoned men?"

Hornigold's gaze swept across the assembled faces, a disquieting stillness in his eyes. It was a void, promising nothing, revealing less. "We fulfill the decree," he stated, his voice a low rumble that seemed to vibrate in the very timbers of the ship. "We meet Vane's vessel head-on. Our ensigns will snap defiance in the wind. That's how we seize him. Drag him back for a reckoning that will echo with the snap of hemp and the final, agonizing stretch of a neck." He paused, the silence thick enough to taste. "A fate we all, in our own ways, have earned."

He wove through the huddled forms, his boots thudding with a deliberate rhythm, drawing him toward the stern where Blair wrestled with the groaning wheel. The wood beneath Blair's calloused hands felt slick with sea spray, the salt stinging his eyes.

"What was that?" Blair's voice, usually a steady baritone, was laced with an edge of unease, the sea-wind snatching at his words. "What madness were you conjuring?"

Hornigold turned, his eyes, still unnervingly empty, met Blair's. "Madness, Blair?"

"That... that whole damn sermon you just preached! The way you carried yourself, it's enough to stir a mutiny that'll swallow this ship whole!" Blair's knuckles were white on the wheel, his breathing shallow, ragged against the roar of the ocean.

"There will be no mutiny on my watch," Hornigold stated, a flat, chilling certainty in his tone. He turned away, his gaze fixing on the churning grey expanse of the sea, as if finding answers in its depths.

"Are you... are you alright?" Blair's voice softened, a tremor running through it, the fear a palpable thing in the salty air.

"I'm more than all right, Blair," Hornigold replied, his voice still distant, laced with an undertow of something... dangerous. "I know precisely what I'm doing."

"You're terrifying the crew!" Blair's voice cracked, a raw accusation. "And me, Hornigold! You're scaring the life out of me!"

The suffocating blackness of a long night bled into the bruised hues of dawn, a drawn-out, agonizing surrender. Hornigold, a silhouette etched against the lightening sky, gripped the salt-crusted wheel like a drowning man clings to driftwood. The air, thick with the brine of the open sea and the metallic tang of anticipation, vibrated with the groaning timbers of The Robert. Then, piercing the haze, a jagged necklace of islands. And there, a predatory shadow against the dawning light, lay Vane's ship, anchored off a jagged point.

Hornigold's hand, calloused and scarred, reached for the spyglass, its cold brass a stark contrast to the feverish heat in his gut. He brought it to his eye; the world sharpened into a brutal focus. Was it The Inferno? Vane's cursed flagship. The confirmation, when it came, was a bitter draught. He lowered the glass, the tremor in his hand betraying the iron will hold him steady. The ship's bell, a clanging summons that tore through the lingering quiet, shattered the peace, a brutal awakening for those who had sought solace on the unforgiving deck.

Blair, a creature of the deck even in slumber, stirred, his rough-spun shirt clinging to his damp skin. He stumbled towards Hornigold, his eyes, still heavy with sleep, sharpened by the captain's unyielding gaze. A tremor ran through the growing assembly of men on deck, a restless surge of energy, a palpable hum of the predator scenting prey.

"What is it, Captain?" Blair's voice, a gravelly rumble, was barely a whisper against the wind.

Hornigold's lips, drawn tight, parted. "We've found our destination." The words were a challenge, a pronouncement.

A flicker of understanding, then a sharp intake of breath. "Vane?"

"Aye," Hornigold spat, the single syllable laced with a history of shared blood and bitter rivalry. "Raise the colors! We don't want any confusion on our hands." The ensign, a defiant splash of color against the grey, unfurled with a snap, a banner of war declared.

The Robert, no longer a ghost in the mist, began its slow, deliberate approach, a predator stalking its wounded prey. The water churned, a restless sea mirroring the turmoil brewing within. As they drew alongside The Inferno, a lone figure on the enemy deck, a sentinel of Vane's domain, bellowed across the expanse of water.

A defiant echo from Hornigold's own deck answered the cry. "Ahoy!"

More figures materialized on the Inferno's deck, a growing knot of menace. And then Vane himself. He strode to the railing, a figure of chilling charisma, his voice carrying across the water. "Is that Hornigold's ship I see?"

The salt spray whipped across Hornigold's weathered face; he made himself visible to the crew of the Inferno. Honor among thieves was not the currency of their trade, but honor among each other, well, that's something different altogether.

"Aye. It is Captain."

Vane emerged, a shadow coalescing from the gloom of his own deck. His eyes, sharp as shards of obsidian, raked over Hornigold. "What business do you have stirring the devil's cauldron out here, old friend?"

Hornigold tasted copper on his tongue, the tang of desperation mingling with the brine. "Do I have the king's own permission to set foot on your infernal vessel?"

A smile spread across Vane's face, a flash of white against the deepening darkness. "The King's permission? You know damn well that ain't the currency we trade in. Bring yourself over here, old man."

Blair, his face a mask of bewildered apprehension, spun to Hornigold, his voice a tight whisper against the groaning timbers. "What are you doing? This is madness."

"I'll go alone," Hornigold growled, the words a low rumble in his chest. The lure of Vane's dangerous charisma was a current he could no longer resist. "I have words for Vane, words that require no ears but his."

Blair's gaze held a mixture of fear and grudging respect. "Then God help you, for you know what you're playing with."

Hornigold's gaze flickered, a brief, almost imperceptible acknowledgment, before he turned, his boots finding the rough, unforgiving grain of the plank. Each step was a gamble, the wood groaning a protest beneath his weight, the abyss below a silent, hungry maw. The air thrummed with unspoken tension as he crossed the chasm, the stench of tar and sweat growing stronger, the raw, untamed energy of The Inferno a palpable force.

He landed on the deck with a thud; the wood vibrating under Vane's steady presence. Vane's eyes, pools of midnight, seemed to bore into Hornigold's very soul. "Well, well, an old salt washed ashore. What tempest blew you so far from familiar waters? I thought you lot were basking in the king's supposed grace, tucked away safe in New Providence." His voice was a silken thread, laced with something dark and knowing. "Did the pardons truly take?"

They moved towards the mainmast, the creak of the ship a constant, mournful song. Hornigold could feel the eyes of Vane's crew upon him, a hundred silent judgments. "Aye. Pardoned. I spoke for all of us," Hornigold said, his voice devoid of triumph, heavy with the weight of his choices. "And I believe I have you to thank for it, Charles."

Vane's smile widened, a dangerous glint in his eyes. "Did you? Did you truly enjoy the taste of that pill?"

The question hung in the air, acrid and sharp. Hornigold felt a knot tighten in his gut, a sense of profound unease. "Not so much," he admitted, the words clipped and raw. He met Vane's gaze, his own burning with an urgent, desperate plea. "May I speak with you in private, Charles? The sea has secrets, and this is no place for eavesdroppers."

The cabin door creaked shut behind them, swallowing the sounds of the ship and its men. Vane turned, his face no longer the mask of an amused predator. A flicker of something akin to concern, or perhaps suspicion, shadowed his features. "Private? What is it that you can't say before my men? Your reputation precedes you, and I'd rather not have them thinking you've gone soft."

Hornigold's breath hitched, the confession a bitter bile in his throat. "We didn't just 'happen' to be here. I was sent. Sent to find you." The words, once spoken, hung in the charged silence, heavy with the foreboding of a storm about to break.

Vane's Promise

"To find me?" The words are surprising, sharp, and accusatory. Vane felt the shift, the subtle tremor of something cracking beneath the surface.

"Don't get yourself riled," Hornigold's voice drawled, a silken whisper laced with a tremor that hinted at something far more dangerous than mere annoyance. This mad venture, from the moment of its conception, clawed at my insides.

A glint, hard and cold, flashed in Vane's eyes. "And what, pray tell, is your intent now?"

A heavy sigh, thick with resignation and something akin to despair, escaped the man's lips. "Nothing. These souls I've marshalled, this collection of desperate faces... they ache for an end to this folly as much as I. I'd hoped, truly hoped, you might lend me a hand."

Vane's jaw tightened, the muscles coiling. "And what impossible favour do you beg of me?"

"I sought New Providence for... for solace. A place to scrub the grime from my soul, to shed the skin of what I'd become. But the sea, it seems, has a long memory. And the ghosts you try to outrun? They have a terrifying knack for finding the scent of your fear."

A guttural laugh, devoid of mirth, erupted from Vane. "Rogers. He sent you. He knows you're the bloodhound who can sniff us out. That… bastard!"

A flicker of something that might have been fear, or perhaps a desperate calculation, crossed the man's features. "Are there any pockets of civilization, any scattered souls clinging to these unforgiving shores?"

"Two, by my reckoning," Vane spat, his voice rough and absolute. "And why does that matter to your plight?"

"I want to give you my ship." Hornigold's words bored a hole inside Vane's conscience.

Vane's eyes, usually sharp and calculating, snapped wide, mirroring the sudden shock that seized him. "You… you what?"

"My ship," the man repeated, his voice cracking with a raw emotion that Vane hadn't expected. "As much as it tears at the very fiber of my being, it is yours. This is the only way I can truly vanish, to become smoke on the wind."

A raw, disbelieving snort escaped Vane. "You must have a king's ransom tucked away, then. To orchestrate such a... a flight."

"Do not trouble your mind with my meagre fortunes," the man said, his gaze suddenly distant, haunted. "My concern is solely for my own soul's desperate scramble."

Vane stared, the sheer audacity of the man washing over him like a rogue wave. A slow, grudging respect, tinged with a primal fear, churned in his gut. "You've got the brass, mate. You've truly got the brass."

"One final, gnawing thing. You'll take Blair. He's crumbling, that old dog. Too brittle for these shadows." Hornigold's voice, a rasp like dry leaves skittering across a tombstone, snagged Vane's attention.

"I give you my oath, Ben. Whether by loyalty, code, or sheer piratical responsibility."

Hornigold, taking in these last few moments, turned to leave. The rough-hewn timbers of Vane's cabin seemed to exhale a rank, forgotten scent.

"Hornigold!" The bark ripped through the tension, sharp as a splinter.

He turned, the dim lamplight catching the glint in his eye, a predatory gleam that hinted at depths Vane would never plumb.

"You… you're great, Captain. Truly. Benjamin Hornigold." Vane's words were sincere, an admiration that clung to the air like a shroud.

Hornigold remained framed in the doorway, the faint light playing across a face etched with a thousand voyages and a hundred thousand regrets. "I am many things, Vane. But 'great'? That's a badge I'll never wear."

"You are. You are, mate." The finality in Vane's declaration was true.

Hornigold didn't reply. He simply dissolved into the swirling, clamoring chaos of the ship's deck. The salty spray stung his face, a familiar, bracing kiss. As he stepped onto the worn planks of The Robert, the crew surged around him, a tempest of rough voices and calloused hands, a living embodiment of the very 'many things' he refused to claim. The air thrummed with their anticipation, a palpable hunger that mirrored the gnawing void within him.

Trade and Blood

The air thrummed with an unspoken tension as Blair, a whirlwind of agitated energy, lunged after Hornigold. His boots, usually a soft whisper on deck, now pounded a frantic rhythm against the worn wood, each beat a desperate plea. The salty tang of the sea, usually invigorating, now seemed to cling to his throat, thick with apprehension.

"Captain!" The word was a ragged gasp, ripped from Blair's chest. "Captain!" His voice cracked, a desperate, reedy sound swallowed by the vastness of the ship. He strained, his eyes sharp, darting, searching for the familiar silhouette of the man who commanded his unwavering loyalty. The scent of tar and brine, usually the comforting perfume of their world, now felt suffocating.

He pushed himself harder, a relentless pursuit against the setting sun that bled crimson across the horizon, mirroring the turmoil churning within him. He needed to reach Hornigold, to anchor himself to the man's presence, before the encroaching darkness consumed them both. "Ben!" The name, once a casual greeting, was now a raw cry, a plea etched with fear and confusion.

They skidded to a halt before the captain's cabin door. Hornigold, nervous and frightened of the unknown, finally turned. The rough wool of his coat seemed to absorb the dim light, making him appear larger, more formidable. His eyes, deep pools reflecting the dying day, held a weariness that cut Blair to the bone.

"I'll explain," Hornigold's voice was a low rumble, a promise that felt as fragile as sea foam.

Inside, the cabin was a sanctuary of disarray. The air grew heavy with the scent of old paper and leather. Hornigold moved with a deliberate grace, a predator preparing for a hunt, his hands sifting through a collection of drawers that held not just belongings, but the tangible remnants of a life about to be discarded.

"What in the devil is happening, Ben?" Blair's voice, normally steady, now quivered, a testament to the seismic shift occurring around him. The crew's whispers, like a swarm of gnats, buzzed at the edges of his hearing, their fear a palpable presence in the confined space. "They think you've lost your mind! They're terrified of losing this newfound freedom, this life we've fought for!"

Hornigold's gaze snapped back, sharp as a cutlass. A steely resolve, a grim acceptance replaced the weariness in his eyes. "And they won't, Mr. Blair."

"Then tell me!" Blair's voice rocketed, a thunderclap in the tense quiet. His knuckles were white where he gripped the edge of a weathered sea chart.

Hornigold's hands stilled. He turned fully, the fading light catching the sharp angles of his face, illuminating a torment that went deeper than any physical wound. "I'm leaving." The words were stark, brutal, stripping away the pretense, the camaraderie, the shared purpose. "I can't bear this weight any longer. I thought... I truly believed there was a path forward, a way to reconcile the man I am with the things I've done. But there's too much of this... this rot within me to betray another man's trust. I'm leaving, Blair. I'm vanishing. Do you understand?"

Blair's breath hitched, a sharp intake of air. His eyes, usually so sharp and discerning, widened to saucers, reflecting the terrifying precipice they now stood upon. The world tilted, and the familiar scent of the sea now carried the bitter undertone of abandonment and a future snatched away before he could even grasp it.

"My God, Ben!" The words ripped from the man's throat, a raw, guttural sound. "You are responsible for this crew! This is your ship! Where are we to go?"

Hornigold's movements were those of a predator's–
swift, efficient. The coarse canvas of his bag brushed
against his leg as he stuffed it with the scent of salt-
worn leather and illicit spices, a faint tremor in his
hands betraying the calculated calm. The heavy
wooden door groaned open, a dark maw swallowing
him as he stepped into the setting Caribbean sun.

"I have given my ship to Vane," his voice, roughened
by sea and sin, echoed across the deck. "I have
ordered that all of you stay on the Robert. And you
won't see me again."

"You're mad, Ben!" a voice, choked with disbelief,
clawed at the air.

"That may well be," Hornigold replied, a ghost of a
smile touching his lips, a smile that didn't reach his
eyes. "But now, I will be truly free. Away from this. It
is my decision. Trust in that."

He moved with deliberate grace, a seasoned wolf
navigating a flock of bewildered sheep. The deck
boards creaked under his worn boots as he made his
way to the ship's center, the cacophony of the crew a
palpable wave crashing against him. He stopped, his
gaze sweeping over their weathered faces, the
desperate hope and simmering fear etched into
every line.

"I know what you all must be thinking."

A voice from the crowd of men cut through the murmur. "Aye. You've gone mad!"

The crew's unrest escalated, a rising tide of mutinous whispers and agitated shuffling. Hornigold raised a hand, a surprisingly commanding gesture, and silence, thick and charged, descended.

"I assure you," he began, his voice dropping to a low, resonant hum that seemed to vibrate in their very bones, "that I am not. I spoke with Vane. He and I… we have an understanding."

Another voice, sharp with suspicion, pierced the quiet. "What kind of understanding?"

Hornigold turned, his eyes, the color of a storm-tossed sea, locking onto the tattered men before him. "I know you don't want to lose your pardons. You won't lose them. I am taking my leave of you, men. I came to New Providence for the same reasons most of you did. To carve out a new life. But as long as England commands us to hunt our own kind, we will never be truly free. Vane understands that. He's agreed. If you want to leave, you can at any time. If you cross paths with any British entanglement, simply tell them you were on a failed errand for Governor Rogers, left to fend for yourselves." A subtle shift in his stance, a tightening of his jaw. "No harm will come to you. You are pardoned. Or," his gaze flickered towards the distant shore, a glint of something unreadable in his eyes, "if you crave the devil's embrace, you can join him. There is strength in numbers, if that is your desire."

He walked towards a long boat, stowed with care, the crew trailing him like shadows. Blair, his face a mask of concern, stepped forward. "Give the captain room. He's made his peace."

Hornigold glanced at a nearby crewman. "Gather another man. Lower this long boat." The man's response was a blur of motion, a testament to the unspoken command.

Across the water, Vane stood, arms crossed, a stoic sentinel. He watched the unfolding drama on The Robert with a stillness that spoke volumes, a silent nod of profound respect. "That's one brave man," he murmured, his voice a low rumble lost in the vastness.

The crew lowered the longboat into the vibrant turquoise of the Caribbean, like a cradle descending, and its creaking offered a mournful protest. The crew lined the ship's rail, a silent, spellbound audience as Hornigold, a solitary figure against the immensity of the sea, climbed in. The boat kissed the water with a gentle splash, the scent of salt and freedom filling the air. He took the oars, his powerful arms a blur of motion as he began to row, his back to the ship, his face turned towards the island.

"How can we find you?" Blair's voice, a desperate plea, cut through the salty breeze.

Hornigold paused, a slow, enigmatic smile spreading across his face. "You won't, James. You won't! It's been a pleasure to see you again, Blair. And Godspeed to you all! Godspeed!" The rhythmic dip of his oars became a solitary pulse, fading into the endless, sun-drenched expanse.

Easy Pickens

The salt spray stung their faces, a cold kiss from the unforgiving sea, as the crews of The Robert and The Inferno stood locked in hushed reverence. Eyes, sharp as a gull's, tracked Hornigold's solitary figure, a silhouette against the bleached sand, as he rowed away from them, far into the unknown. The rhythmic splash of his oars was the only sound, a dirge for a life shed. Then, a slow, agonizing descent. His ship's flag, a proud banner of defiance moments before, dipped to half-mast, the black silk surrendering to the wind.

Hornigold, a phantom already, breathed a silent farewell. Not just to the weathered timbers that had been his kingdom, but to the very marrow of his bones, to a life that had been both his chains and his wings, now finally released into the boundless sky. On the Robert, a collective gasp, a tremor of respect that ran through the hardened men. Men lifted hats with rough hands clutching worn felt and held them to their chests, which had known countless battles, silently acknowledging a man walking into his own legend.

Six months had bled into the colonial consciousness since Hornigold had vanished. And in that echoing silence, the myth of Blackbeard had blossomed, a dark flower, its tendrils strangling every settlement, town, and whispered rumor. Now, on the blood-soaked deck of his own vessel, Blackbeard, a titan of shadow and sea-fury, stood sentinel at the helm. His gaze, a hawk's piercing stare, swept the horizon through a polished spyglass. A smudge appeared, flourishing. A merchant ship, plump and unsuspecting, sailed towards them like a lamb to the slaughter. He lowered the glass, the polished brass cool against his calloused palm. He turned to his helmsman, a grin as sharp and predatory as a shark's splitting his face.

"Look at them," his voice, a gravelly rumble that promised oblivion, dripped with dark amusement. "Unsuspecting. Oblivious to the storm gathering on their horizon."

The helmsman, his knuckles white on the wheel, offered a nervous chuckle. "It's getting to be too easy, Captain."

Blackbeard's eyes narrowed, the amusement hardening into something colder. "What did I tell you, lads? No fuss. No mess. A clean sweep."

Israel Hands, taking in his own survey of the situation, his shadow long and lean. "Should we prime the guns, Captain?"

A slow, deliberate smile spread across Blackbeard's lips, revealing a confidence that refused to be challenged. "Have we ever?"

"No, sir," Hands conceded, a tremor in his voice, a premonition he couldn't shake. "But I have a feeling..."

Blackbeard leaned in, the scent of victory and gunpowder clinging to him. "That our lucky streak is going to run out?"

"Aye, Captain," Hands confirmed, the word heavy with unspoken dread.

Blackbeard studied him for a long moment, his keen eyes probing the depths of his first mate's unease. "Very well, Mr. Hands. Put powder to the guns. Softly. Hand out extra pistols to the men."

Blackbeard's brow furrowed. "Does that... satisfy your worries?"

A genuine smile, laced with a dangerous amusement, returned to Israel's face. " Very much indeed."

With a renewed sense of purpose, Israel turned, his gait purposeful, towards a small arms case. The clatter of metal against wood echoed across the deck as he pulled out pistols, each one a promise of swift violence. The crew, their faces grim, their eyes alight with a shared understanding of the dance that was about to begin, formed a silent, expectant line. They knew the drill. They knew the weight of the extra steel now resting in their hands. And Blackbeard, the very embodiment of the coming tempest, remained by the wheel, a colossus against the churning sea, the anticipation a palpable thrumming in the air.

"Never, Captain, have I witnessed a scheme so utterly brilliant, so ripe for the taking!"

Blackbeard's eyes, like chips of obsidian glinting with a predatory fire, met Israel's. "In the savage theater of war," he rumbled, his voice a low growl that vibrated in the salt-laced air, "one must don the velvet glove to hide the iron fist. And they, poor fools, see only the velvet."

"They suspect nothing. I almost feel sorry for them." Israel breathed, a grin splitting his weathered face.

"Precisely. The Revenge, in their shallow eyes, is naught but a lumbering merchant ship, a harmless vessel laden with... what? Spices? Silk? They taste only the illusion, and soon they shall choke on the reality."

A guttural bellow, a roar of eager anticipation, sliced through the tension. "The men are ready, Captain!"

Israel's voice, a rough instrument honed by countless raids, echoed across the deck.

Blackbeard's gaze, sharp and unyielding, swept over his assembled fiends. "Then let them taste the wind, Israel. Stand by."

The Rose, a creature of innocent commerce, drifted closer, her sails catching the deceptive breeze. Her crew, oblivious to the storm brewing on the horizon, paced their decks with the carefree arrogance of the unsuspecting. Blackbeard, a shadow moving with unnerving grace, descended to the main deck, the very air seeming to crackle around him. The Revenge, a coiled viper, surged alongside the unsuspecting merchantman, her broadside a thunderous declaration. The Rose's crew, drawn by the sudden proximity, clustered at the railing, their faces a tableau of mild curiosity.

A cheerful, unsuspecting hail drifted across the water. "Ahoy!"

Israel's reply, laced with a chilling hint of amusement, boomed back. "Ahoy!"

A pregnant silence descended, thick and suffocating, as the two vessels lay juxtaposed. Then, like a phantom erupting from the very heart of the crowd, Blackbeard appeared. His voice, no longer a rumble

but a cataclysmic explosion, tore through the quiet.
"FIRE!"

The command, a thunderclap of pure savagery,
unleashed a symphony of destruction. Without a
flicker of hesitation, the crew of The Revenge, a
whirlwind of black powder and cold steel, unleashed
a torrent of fire–not at the men, but just above their
heads. The sickening whiz of lead ripped through the
air, a prelude to the unfolding horror.

A horrifying, domino-like cascade of bodies toppled
from the railing. Screams, raw and animalistic, tore
from the throats of the merchant sailors as they
scrambled for nonexistent cover, their once-proud
stances dissolving into pathetic attempts to escape
the impossible.

Blackbeard, his boots crunching on the splintered
wood, strode to the helm, the very embodiment of
absolute authority. The grating shriek of grappling
hooks filled the air as Blackbeard's men, with
practiced brutality, hurled their iron claws. The Rose
lurched violently, drawn into the crushing embrace
of The Revenge. Roars of triumph, primal and
exultant, erupted from the throats of Blackbeard's
devoted legion. He drew his cutlass, its polished
steel catching the dying sunlight, and raised it
towards the beleaguered merchantman.

"Do you feel that?" His voice, a primal scream of unadulterated dominion, echoed across the water. "THAT IS POWER! The raw, unfettered power of the sea and the sword!"

He turned, his gaze burning holes through the billowing smoke that now wreathed the ships, a testament to the chaos he had unleashed. He strode towards a dangling rope, a predator leaping into his domain. With a powerful surge, he swung across the chasm, landing on the deck of The Rose with the grace of a panther, his eyes already scanning for his next conquest.

Blackbeard moved swiftly and descended into the bowels of the ship, the air heavy with the stench of fear and stale sweat. Below, in the suffocating darkness of the hold, his crew stood sentinel, their pistols trained on the terrified faces of The Rose's captured sailors, their breath ragged whispers in the oppressive silence.

Raise The Black

The stale air in the hold of The Rose was palpable. Blackbeard's Bosun, a mountain of a man with eyes like chipped flint, turned to address him. The guttural rasp of his voice cut through the creaking of the timbers and the groaning of the sea.

"All hands accounted for, Captain. The prize… It's handsome."

Blackbeard's gaze, a dark tempest of a thousand captured horizons, swept across the groaning hull. A low, predatory rumble vibrated in his chest.

"A handsome cargo indeed," he murmured, the words laced with the promise of plunder and the shadow of damnation.

He moved with predatory grace, each step resonating with an unseen authority. He stopped before the captured crew, a collection of trembling souls huddled like frightened sheep. Their eyes, wide and glazed with terror, darted from one hulking pirate to another. The metallic clank of cutlasses seemed to echo the frantic pounding of their hearts.

"Where," Blackbeard's voice dropped, a silken menace that coiled around them like a serpent, "were you taking this bounty?"

Silence, thick and suffocating, descended. The only sound was the insistent, mocking roar of the ocean. He leaned in, his shadow falling over them like a shroud, the faint scent of rum and something darker, something ancient and terrible, clinging to him.

"Speak!" The command was not a shout, but a thunderclap that cracked the very air.

A scrawny figure, his skin stretched taut over bone, swallowed hard. His voice, a reedy whisper against the gale, finally emerged, laced with a desperate plea. "We... we were sailing to Bath Town, sir."

Blackbeard's head tilted, his brow furrowing, not in confusion, but in chilling amusement. "Bath Town?" he repeated, the name rolling off his tongue like a curse.

The sailor, a rat caught in the glare of a hawk, could only nod, his Adam's apple bobbing frantically. "Aye, sir. North Carolina."

A slow, cruel smile spread across Blackbeard's face, splitting his scarred visage. He turned his piercing gaze upon his own hardened crew, a silent communion of beasts of the sea, before snapping his attention back to the trembling captive. The promise of a bloody reckoning, a feast of fear and despair, hung heavy in the salt-laden air.

"Please, sir. What... what becomes of us?" The plea, a desperate whisper against the creak and groan of the battered vessel. Blackbeard's smile, a flash of gold and malice, was not a comfort, but a predator's baring of teeth. It promised not salvation, but a terrifying, untamed freedom.

"A long row in a longboat." Blackbeard's answer was absolute. Israel Hands materialized from the shadows behind Blackbeard. "Your orders, Captain?" His voice was a low rumble.

Blackbeard turned, the firelight from a nearby lantern glinting in his eyes, turning them into molten pools of ambition. "Take these men," he commanded, his voice a guttural roar that vibrated through the deck, "and load them up. The cargo is ours. The ship," he spat the words, a venomous hiss, "she'll find her sandy grave at the bottom." He turned, a titan of shadow and fury, and strode towards the stairs leading to the main deck, the wood groaning beneath his weight. Israel followed, a shadow attached to a hurricane.

"You... you don't want the ship?" Israel's voice, laced with a desperate confusion, was barely audible above the wind's mournful cry. "Don't we need another vessel?"

Blackbeard's stride didn't falter. His gaze was fixed on some unseen horizon, a phantom destination etched in his mind. "Not where we're going. A second ship," he sneered, the sound like grinding stones, "is a leash. It drags. We travel unburdened."

Israel scrambled to keep pace, the salt spray kissing his face, stinging his eyes. "And where, then, are we bound?"

They reached the main deck, the vast expanse of worn timber a stage for their grim pronouncements. They moved to the edge, the heaving sea a vast, indifferent maw below.

"Where they were," Blackbeard declared, his voice echoing with the confidence of commerce. "Bath Town."

"Bath Town?" Israel's brow furrowed, a flicker of unease crossing his hardened features. "Where the hell is that?"

Blackbeard's smile returned, wider, more terrifying this time. The wind whipped his wild hair, lending him an almost demonic aura. "A sleepy little place," he breathed, the words a promise of pillaging, "ripe... ripe for the reaping." The currency was cargo, not gold or silver, and quick cash was better than months of waiting for the Spanish to send a treasure galleon to these shores. Hurricane season had arrived, and "Blackbeard" was the only storm that troubled the waters.

The air crackled with tension as Blackbeard, a monstrous silhouette against the bruised twilight sky, spun to confront Israel. Behind him, a tide of his men, a snarling pack of wolves, herded the broken remnants of the captured crew, their moans a low thrum beneath the rising wind.

"See to these curs for now." Blackbeard's voice, a rumble of thunder, cut through the salt-laced air.

Israel, a flicker of weary resignation in his eyes, let out a guttural sigh that seemed to carry the weight of a thousand storms. "Aye." He turned his back on the formidable captain, his silhouette swallowed by the gloom as he strode towards the far side of the doomed Rose, where a longboat, like a starved predator, was being lowered into the heaving sea.

With a primal roar, Blackbeard launched himself, a shadow detaching from the deck, swinging on a thick rope towards the sturdy bulk of The Revenge.

Israel, his movements precise and brutal, directed his own men. The scent of fear, sharp and acrid, hung heavy as they shoved the terrified souls from The Rose into the waiting longboat. "Israel!" Blackbeard's voice boomed again, a demand that vibrated in the timbers of the ship. "Get their cargo to The Revenge! And leave a keg of powder in the gut of their ship! We'll send them on their way with a proper send-off!"

Blackbeard moved like a storm front, a mountain of menace ascending to the stern, where his steersman, a weathered gargoyle, awaited his command at the helm. His calloused hands still polishing the brass of the compass, his gaze sharp and knowing, looked up. "A fine day's work, Captain."

Blackbeard's broad-brimmed hat came off, a brief respite from the biting wind as he wiped a bead of sweat from his brow. The hat, a crown of dread, was rammed back into place. "You can say that again, you old sea dog!" Deep within the hold, a lone figure, one of Blackbeard's trusted hounds, grunted with effort, rolling a heavy barrel of powder. The scent of the volatile powder, a promise of oblivion, filled the air. He scrambled out, a phantom moving through the belly of the beast, his urgency a palpable thing as he burst onto the main deck.

Blackbeard's eyes, burning coals in the encroaching darkness, fixed on The Rose as it began its desperate, agonizing retreat. The crewman, a blur of motion, raced to a rope, a fleeting bridge between damnation and survival, and swung across to The Revenge. The watching crew of The Revenge held their breath, a collective predator poised to strike.

"Fire at will!" Blackbeard's order, a lightning strike, ripped through the night.

A row of cannons, their maws gaping and dark, were dragged to the port windows. As the command echoed, rough hands yanked at the primer cords. A thunderous boom that shook the very foundations of their world followed a deafening crack, a visceral tearing of the air. The cannons recoiled, their fiery breath exhaled.

Blackbeard and his men watched, a chillingly serene audience, as iron death tore into the hull of The Rose. Splinters, like jagged teeth, ripped through its wooden flesh. Then, a monstrous blast erupted through its main deck. The mainmast, a once proud tower, groaned and toppled, crashing onto the bow. The ship bled seawater, succumbing to the gnawing hunger of the Atlantic.

In the small longboat, the crew of The Rose, their faces contorted with terror, threw themselves down, trying to shield themselves from the lethal confetti of splintered wood that rained down around them. They watched; the unforgiving ocean swallowed their hearts, a drumbeat of despair.

Israel, a ghost in the carnage, walked back to the stern, his steps measured, as Blackbeard stood, a titan gazing at the smoldering ruins. "Captain!" Israel's call, laced with an unnerving calm, sliced through the roar of the waves. Blackbeard turned; his eyes, ancient and full of fire, met Israel's. "The Carolinas? That's a bold stroke, even for us, wouldn't you say?"

A slow grin, a fissure in Blackbeard's formidable face, spread. "Aye, it is. And any chance I get to spit in England's eye, you know I'll take it."

Coastal Catastrophe

The reek of salt and sweat clung to the air as Israel's laughter, a raw, guttural sound, scraped against the creak of the hull. "Those farmers won't mind!" he crowed, the words a promise laced with venom, as if conjured from the very spray that lashed their weathered faces. Blackbeard's answering smile was a flash of predatory white against the shadow of his beard, a darkness that seemed to swallow the very light. His voice, a rumble that vibrated through the timbers, dripped with chilling amusement. "We'll give them a good reason to tolerate us!" he growled, the syllables like cannon fire. He spun, the glint of his cutlass catching the dim lantern light, his eyes, sharp as a hawk's, locking onto his steersman. "Five points northeast!"

A sharp, almost eager "Aye!" crackled from the steersman, his hands already wrestling the heavy wheel, the groaning wood a prelude to the storm they were about to unleash.

Meanwhile, in Virginia, the air in Governor Spotswood's office was thick with an unfamiliar tension. The opulent room, usually a sanctuary of refined power, now crackled with a barely suppressed fury. Spotswood, a man carved from mahogany and authority, his regal bearing amplified by the gleam of polished spectacles perched on his aquiline nose, slammed the paper down onto his vast, claw-footed desk. The headline, a stark declaration of their vulnerability, "BLACKBEARD STRIKES TRADE ROUTES" seemed to writhe beneath his fist. The polished surface shuddered, echoing the tremor of his rage. Sunlight, fractured by the grand windows that framed the unforgiving coastline, painted stark stripes across the concerned faces of the British soldiers and dignitaries who stood, hushed and expectant.

"A slap in the face?!" Spotswood roared, the words a raw wound ripped open. As he rose, his movements were sharp and decisive, the stiff fabric of his coat whispering like an angry accusation. He stalked to the window, his reflection a distorted image in the glass, a man teetering on the precipice of war. He turned, his eyes burning with a cold, furious fire, and swept across the assembled room.

"My God, what inferno have you men fallen into? You stand there, statues carved from indifference, while Blackbeard, that swaggering, salt-crusted fiend, gorges himself on our very lifeblood! Do you not feel the gnawing emptiness in your bellies, the chill that seeps into your bones from empty larders? This is not some petty theft, you fool; this is a deliberate throttling of our spirit!"

'He, this phantom of the docks, brazenly intercepts the bounty meant for our hands, the sustenance that whispers promises of survival. And for what? To peddle it back to us, to the very people he bleeds dry, with a twisted mockery of a "tax-free" boon! A gift from the wolf to the lamb, while England, our sovereign, sharpens its sword, ready to levy its own cruel tribute upon our already broken backs!" Spotswood paces about the room. The weight of England's wrath on his shoulders.

"Explain this to me! How can you watch our future being plundered, taste the bitter ashes of despair on the wind, and still your hearts beat with such placid stillness! Does the rot not sting your nostrils? Does the silence of our children's hunger not scream in your ears? Tell me, men, what phantom comfort holds you captive while your very souls are being devoured?" Silence falls around the room. What could be said? The truth of the matter was laid out, and no one could dispute that.

 Lieutenant Robert Maynard, a man etched with the grim resolve of the Royal Navy, squared his shoulders. His voice, though strained, cut through the oppressive silence.

"Governor, the Royal Navy has scoured every crevice of the Caribbean. The stench of unchecked piracy has clouded every lead, rendering this quarry maddeningly elusive."

Governor Spotswood, his face a thundercloud, slammed a fist onto the mahogany desk, the resonant thud echoing the fury building within him. His eyes, sharp as a barracuda's, bored into Maynard.

"He is not in the Caribbean, Lieutenant! He is breathing the very air of our waters!"

Maynard flinched; the governor's raw fury was a physical blow. "Governor, our strength is depleted. We simply lack the manpower to pursue such a ghost. And England, sir, will not dispatch further resources until we can demonstrably prove the substantial, tangible threat this brigand poses... here."

Spotswood, a predator scenting weakness, snatched a crumpled newspaper from his desk. With a savage flourish, he dangled it before Maynard's face, the paper crumpled, the sensational headline screaming silently.

"Then tell me, Lieutenant, what is this news I hold in my trembling hand? Is this not a blazing testament to his insidious presence? Does it not burn with undeniable proof of his venomous infestation?"

Maynard recoiled, his gaze fixed on the accusatory print, an icy dread seeping into his gut. Spotswood, his lip curled in a sneer, lowered the paper, the phantom threat momentarily receding.

"If the Crown refuses to bolster our ranks," he began, his voice dropping to a dangerous murmur, "then we must forge them ourselves. Lieutenant, I recall you possess a brother... a Captain, is he not?"

A collective breath hitched in the room. Every gaze, heavy with expectation, pinned Maynard. He felt the weight of their scrutiny, the unspoken demand pressing down like the crushing depths of the sea. He swallowed, the rough wool of his uniform scratching his throat.

"Yes, Governor," he conceded, his voice barely a whisper.

Spotswood, a puppet master pulling the strings of fate, resumed his pacing, his footsteps a drumbeat against the polished floorboards. He stopped, his back to Maynard, his silhouette a menacing monolith.

"And where, Lieutenant, is this esteemed brother presently stationed?" The question hung in the air, laced with the promise of consequence, the chilling prelude to a storm gathering just beyond the horizon.

Trade or Trade

Lieutenant Moore, a man whose very presence etched a grim determination onto his face, the seasoned veteran of countless skirmishes, choked out the words, "New Providence." The salt-laced wind whipped his thin hair across eyes that had seen too much, yet still held a spark of unyielding resolve. They had dispatched him to that forgotten outpost, and a gnawing unease already coiled in his gut.

Spotswood's smile was a sharp, predatory gleam that flashed across his lips, a chilling counterpoint to the flickering torchlight that danced in his pupils. He met Maynard's gaze, a silent, potent understanding passing between them, a shared knowledge of the brutal calculus that governed their world. "Perfect," he rasped, his voice a low growl that seemed to vibrate through the very timbers of the ship. "I'll dispatch a courier this instant to Governor Rogers, our newly gained governor. I trust he has the... appropriate disposition... to ensure this venture proceeds with the utmost efficiency. He will undoubtedly keep this approach." The unspoken threat hung heavy in the air, thicker than the storm clouds gathering on the horizon.

The Queen Anne's Revenge, a leviathan of scarred timbers and grim promise, groaned as it clawed its way into Bath Town's harbor. A tide of shadow spilled onto the docks as Blackbeard's men disembarked, a brutal ballet of coiled muscles and eyes that had witnessed too much hell to blink. They were a blight upon the neat, ordered port, their presence a jarring discord in the salty air, their rough-spun clothes a stark contrast to the crisp linen of the townsfolk who recoiled.

Then, a silhouette against the bruised sky, Blackbeard himself descended the gangplank. Each step was a deliberate assertion of dominion, a physical manifestation of the storm he commanded. The air crackled with his approach.

A figure detached itself from the murmuring crowd– the Harbormaster. He was a creature of dust and neglected corners, his unkempt form a testament to a life spent in the shadow of bigger things. His eyes, sharp and darting, fixed on the approaching monolith of Blackbeard. As the Captain moved through his men, a gust of wind carrying the scent of brine and gunpowder, the Harbormaster scurried forward, a mouse before a wolf.

"Good day," the Harbormaster squeaked, his voice thin against the growing tension. "Are you the captain of this... vessel?"

Blackbeard stopped, a predator surveying its prey. A smile, a chillingly devoid thing that promised no warmth, stretched across his scarred face. It was a glimpse into an abyss. "Aye," he rumbled, the sound like stones grinding together. "That I am."

The harbormaster fumbled for his ledger, the worn leather a shield against an intangible threat. His hands, stained with ink and worry, trembled as he opened it. "I... I need to document your name and vessel in the record, sir."

Blackbeard's hand, thick as a sail rope, settled on the hilt of his cutlass. The other rested, almost casually, against his chest, a silent, deadly reminder of the power coiled within him. "Of course," he purred, the sound laced with something akin to amusement, yet utterly devoid of mirth. "I am known as Captain Edward Teach. But to those who respect the fear I sow," his gaze narrowed, "you may call me... Blackbeard."

The quill slipped from the Harbormaster's grasp, clattering onto the wood. His eyes, wide as saucers, locked onto Blackbeard's; a primal terror seized him. He tasted the metallic tang of it in his own mouth.

"You... you dropped your pen," Blackbeard observed, his voice dangerously soft.

"Yes... yes, sir," the Harbormaster stammered, his breath catching in his throat.

"Well," Blackbeard continued, his shadow lengthening as the sun dipped lower, casting the port in an ominous twilight. "What is the fee for docking at your... humble port?"

The harbormaster stood frozen, a statue carved from dread. The ledger lay forgotten at his feet. "No... no fee," he choked out, a reluctant, sickly smile twisting his features.

"Ah!" Blackbeard's smile widened, a predatory baring of teeth. "Most kind. Much obliged for waving the expense." The unspoken threat, however, hung heavy in the air, a tangible weight that pressed down on the Harbormaster, on the town, on everything.

Eden's Garden Parlay

The shadow of Blackbeard, vast and imposing, fell upon the harbormaster. A guttural rumble escaped the pirate's throat as his colossal hand, calloused and scarred, descended like a thunderclap onto the man's shoulder. The harbormaster, a gaunt figure with eyes like frightened mice, recoiled as if struck by lightning, a strangled gasp tearing from his chest.

"A thousand thanks, good sir," Blackbeard rasped, his voice a tempest of gravel and sea salt.

Behind him, a legion of Blackbeard's ruffians, a motley collection of scarred faces and glinting cutlasses, advanced like a tidal wave. Their eyes, sharp and predatory, raked over the Harbormaster, each gaze a silent threat. Then, the Bosun, a hulking brute with a voice like a foghorn, spat a venomous growl, "Move it, you rat!"

The harbormaster, his meager frame vibrating with terror, let out a piercing, high-pitched shriek, a sound utterly incongruous with his supposed authority, and sprang back with the agility of a cornered rabbit. A wave of booming laughter, savage and unrestrained, erupted from Blackbeard's men, echoing through the docks like the baying of hounds.

As Blackbeard and his infamous crew swaggered onto the main thoroughfare of Bath, a hush fell over the townsfolk. Faces, once etched with mundane concerns, contorted in primal fear. The air thickened with the stench of stale rum and unwashed bodies, a stark contrast to the scent of lavender and freshly baked bread that usually perfumed the street. Mothers, their faces pale as parchment, snatched their children close, their hands clamped over innocent eyes, and scurried away, their footsteps a frantic patter on the cobblestones.

Blackbeard halted, his massive frame turning with a deliberate slowness that seemed to stretch the very fabric of time. He surveyed his men, a glint of amusement in his sea-worn eyes. "These are 'tender shoots,' me hearties," he boomed, his voice carrying over the panicked whispers. "No need to soil our hands with anything more than a pleasant stroll. Yet."

All of Bath, from the smallest urchin to the most dignified elder, fixed their eyes on the pirates. They continued their procession, the rhythmic clatter of their boots a stark drumbeat against the silence, until their gaze fell upon a sign creaking in the salty breeze: FLOUNDER'S ALE HOUSE AND INN.

"Let's see if this establishment can quench a pirate's thirst with something more potent than seawater," Blackbeard rumbled, a predatory smile stretching his lips.

The following dawn painted the harbor in soft, pearly hues. Israel, his gaze sharp and unwavering, oversaw the crew as they unloaded the bounty of their recent plunder onto the dock. The only sounds were the mournful cries of gulls and the ceaseless murmur of waves caressing the shore.

Blackbeard approached Israel, his shadow falling long and distorted across the weathered planks. "Separate the victuals from the finery, Israel," he commanded, his voice a low growl that held an undercurrent of iron. "Dispatch men to every settlement from here to Cape Hatteras. They'll peddle our wares out front, and a few coins to those who keep their eyes conveniently averted will ensure smooth sailing."

"Aye, Captain," Israel replied, his voice steady. "Where will you direct your own course?"

Blackbeard's smile widened, revealing a flash of gold teeth. "I have an appointment with the Governor. A small matter of personal enrichment to discuss."

A wry chuckle escaped Israel. "Just try not to send him to the depths, Captain. He might owe us for his funeral."

Blackbeard met Israel's gaze, a shared understanding passing between them. Then, with a final, lingering look at his crew, he turned and strode towards the heart of the town, the very air seeming to ripple in his wake. Israel, his attention drawn back to the task at hand, bellowed to the men on the dock, his voice cutting through the morning air, "To work, ye scurvy dogs! There are riches to be made, and the sea waits for no man!"

The very timbers of the Governor's mansion shuddered, a raw, guttural thunder erupting from Blackbeard's knuckles as they slammed against the ornate oak. Four violent assaults, each a promise of the tempest to come. A moment of strained silence, then a tremor in the stillness, the rasp of a bolt drawn back, the creak of the heavy door yielding a sliver.

"Who calls at such an unholy hour?" A voice, thin and reedy, laced with a tremor of fear, sliced through the pre-dawn chill. Two eyes, wide and darting like trapped sparrows, flickered through the narrow gap, reflecting the grim silhouette that loomed beyond.

Blackbeard, a mountain of shadow and sinew, pressed closer, the scent of brine and gun smoke clinging to him like a second skin. His voice, a low growl that vibrated in the very marrow of the listener, resonated with a dangerous calm. "Captain Teach," he declared, the name a curse, and a legend whispered on the wind. "I have matters of utmost urgency to impart to your Governor."

The rasping sound from within intensified, a choked gasp swallowed by the sudden intrusion of another voice. Deeper, richer, but edged with a distinct unease. "And who, pray tell, disturbs my slumber?" Governor Charles Eden materialized in the dim light, his bulk a soft, pillowy presence against the dark wood, his nightclothes rumpled and damp, as if with sweat. The opulent chamber behind him, glimpsed through the widening crack, hinted at a life of pampered indulgence, a stark contrast to the brutal presence that now commanded his doorstep. His eyes, small and beady, met Blackbeard's, and in their depths, a flicker of primal terror ignited.

"Who is it, Margaret?" The accusation hung in the air, thick with unspoken dread.

The housemaid's eyes, pools of terror, flickered from the looming darkness beyond the opening door to Eden's face, a mask of strained composure. Her voice, a thin thread of fear, whispered, "It's a... Captain Teach, sir. He wishes to speak with you."

"At this hour?" Eden's voice cracked, a desperate plea against the inevitable.

The door groaned open, a ravenous maw revealing a figure that seemed to absorb the very light. Governor Eden staggered back, his breath catching in his throat. Before him stood a legend.

Blackbeard, a silhouette against the night, doffed his hat, a gesture of mock civility that sent shivers down Eden's spine. The metal gleamed dully in the dim light, reflecting not courtesy, but the glint of sharpened steel. "Ah, Governor Eden," his voice rumbled, laced with something akin to amusement, a low growl. "It is a pleasure beyond measure to finally make your acquaintance."

Eden's eyes, wide and stark with dawning horror, darted over the imposing figure. The man was a walking arsenal, pistols strapped across his chest like badges of infamy, his sword a wicked promise at his hip. His gaze met Eden's, a predatory gleam that promised dominion. Eden stammered, his carefully constructed facade crumbling, "Wh-what can I possibly do for you, Captain?"

He reached out a trembling hand, the touch of Blackbeard's calloused palm a searing brand against his skin. "I've come," Blackbeard declared, his words carrying the weight of a thousand cannons, "to speak with you about a... business opportunity, Governor."

The unspoken threat was palpable, a storm gathering on the horizon. "I trust you'll grant me a moment to... collect myself," Eden choked out, a desperate plea for time he knew he wouldn't get.

Eden spun to his housemaid, his voice a strained command. "Margaret, escort Captain Teach to the garden. And see that some tea is prepared for us." The words were a flimsy raft against a tidal wave of fear. As Eden turned away, the housemaid, her face a portrait of petrified compliance, led the notorious pirate through the hushed halls, each step of Blackbeard's boots echoing like a death knell.

In the garden, the night air hung heavy with the scent of damp earth and unspoken tension. Blackbeard sat, a coiled viper, as the housemaid, her hands shaking so violently the teapot rattled, poured tea. Her eyes, wide with primal fear, flitted between the steaming liquid and the monstrous man before her, one moment a flicker of dread, the next a desperate prayer for escape. Blackbeard offered a slow, unnerving smile, a flash of white against his weathered face, and winked. A visceral shudder rippled through her, a primal revulsion. At that precise moment, Eden emerged, his steps hesitant, his face ghastly white, and sank into the chair opposite Blackbeard, the weight of the world pressing down on his shoulders.

Dead Men Tell No Tales

The damp earth clung to Eden's shoes, a primal scent mingling with the sharper, floral notes of his meticulously manicured rose bushes. A faint mist, still clinging to the dawn, kissed his skin. "My apologies for the delay," he murmured, his voice a practiced calm that belied the knot of apprehension tightening in his gut.

A shadow detached itself from the dawn's embrace, the air around it seeming to crackle with an unseen energy. "No apology is necessary, Governor," the voice resonated, a low rumble that vibrated in Eden's chest. "I find your garden… remarkably soothing. A welcome respite before we discuss… matters of consequence." Teach stepped fully into view, a figure that commanded attention not just with his imposing frame, but with an aura of untamed power. "I suspect you know precisely who I am."

Eden felt a prickle on his neck, the subtle shift in the air like the approach of a storm. He met Blackbeard's gaze, the Governor's own eyes, once bright with the morning, now holding a chilling stillness. "Your reputation precedes you, Captain. I have… heard whispers."

"The roar of true power, Governor, often drowns whispers out," Blackbeard said, a wolfish grin stretching across his face, revealing teeth that were perhaps a shade too sharp. He gestured vaguely towards the distant, huddled roofs of the town, a stark contrast to the opulence of the Governor's estate. "I have seen your town, Governor. It is a place starving for life. A hollow shell waiting to be filled."

A guttural laugh, devoid of mirth, escaped Blackbeard. "And as we speak, my fleet has arrived, bringing with it not just supplies, but the very lifeblood this town craves. We are here to carve our fortunes from its desolation. We are here to prosper."

Eden's hand tightened on his gardening shears, the cold metal a stark contrast to the sudden heat in his palms. "And what is it you desire from me, Captain?"

Blackbeard's smile widened, a predatory gleam in his eyes. "A small token of appreciation, Governor. A gesture of good faith." From beneath his weathered coat, he produced a sack. It was heavy, and as he placed it on the polished stone table between them, the metallic clink of coins sent a shiver down Eden's spine. The scent of old gold, mingled with the salty tang of the sea and something else, something vaguely metallic and dangerous, wafted towards him. "All I ask is that you look the other way. That you grant us... our anonymity. Your silence, Governor, is the price of this little contribution."

Eden swallowed, the words tasting like ash. "I wish for no... disruptions in my town, Captain."

"Nor do we, Governor. We are businessmen, after all. We are efficient and... discreet.

"So, you are admitting to peddling... pilfered wares?" Eden's voice was strained, the carefully constructed calm beginning to fray at the edges. "Goods destined for these very shores, no doubt?"

"Aye," Blackbeard confirmed, the word a rough caress. "And for others, no doubt. The common folk, Governor, will hardly notice the absence of burdensome taxes on the necessities they so desperately crave. They will thank us, in their own way, for this... liberation."

Eden's gaze flickered towards the distant horizon, imagining the imposing sails of Blackbeard's ships. "England will not be so... understanding. They will discover this enterprise with haste."

Blackbeard let out another rumbling laugh, this one more genuine, though no less chilling. "Over time, perhaps. But this is a small, forgotten corner of their empire, Governor. As long as things remain… quiet, you need not trouble yourself with the distant pronouncements of kings and queens. Let them believe their grip is iron. We know better." The glint in his eyes, as he met Eden's, was unadulterated avarice, a promise of both immense reward and swift retribution.

The rough-hewn wood of the small table groaned under the sudden, immense pressure as Blackbeard hefts himself to his feet. His shadow, a jagged thing, swallows Eden whole, a tangible weight in the air.

"There's a saying amongst my kind, Governor," his voice rumbled, a low growl like the churning of a tempestuous sea. "One you might do well to etch into your very bones. 'Dead men tell no tales. 'He leans in, his weathered face a roadmap of a thousand storms, his eyes, dark and unfathomable, pinning Eden. "Heard it before, have we?"

Eden's breath hitched, a thin, reedy sound. "I believe I have."

Blackbeard's hand, calloused and bearing the faint scent of salt and something wild, drifts towards the table, not quite touching it. "Then understand this, Governor. Don't make me have to revisit this intimate conversation. *Comprende*?" The unspoken threat hangs in the humid air, thick as gunpowder smoke.

Eden's gaze, wide and swimming with a raw, primal fear, snaps upward. His face, already pale, seemed to drain of all color. He's trapped, a mouse before a hawk.

"It... it seems I have no recourse," Eden whispers, his voice a ragged thread.

A flicker, perhaps amusement, perhaps something far more dangerous, danced in Blackbeard's eyes. He straightens, the sheer force of his presence radiating outwards. "Worry not, Governor. Your skin, and the skins of your meek flock, are safe. As far as the world will ever know, this... exchange... never happened." The promise, delivered with the chilling finality of a cannon blast, offered no solace.

Blackbeard begins his egress, a monolith moving through the garden. He halts, the sudden stillness more unnerving than any movement, and turns, his silhouette stark against the fading light.

"Governors, it seems, have a penchant for dispensing pardons these days," he muses, a dangerous glint in his gaze. "Perhaps you can find it in your heart, Governor, to offer one to a humble sailor. I'll endeavor to find my own way out. No need to trouble yourselves."

He strides away, disappearing into the cavernous maw of the house, leaving Eden adrift in a sea of his own fear. The man remains seated, the echo of Blackbeard's terrifying presence clinging to him like damp sea mist. His eyes fell upon the small, rough pouch of gold, a king's ransom for a moment of terror, and he let out a ragged sigh, the sound of a man who has narrowly escaped the abyss.

Down on the grimy, salt-stained planks of Bath Town's docks, the thunderous rhythm of labor filled the air. The Queen Anne's Revenge, a beast of the sea, groaned as pirates disgorged its stolen bounty. Israel oversaw the chaos, his sharp eyes missing nothing. Then, he saw it–the unmistakable, imposing figure of Blackbeard striding towards them.

"Captain!" Israel's roar cut through the din, a clear signal of deference.

Blackbeard moved with an unnerving grace, his boots striking the planks with a resonant thud. He approached Israel, the scent of his passage a heady mix of brine, sweat, and something undeniably predatory.

Israel's grin was a flash of white against his tanned face. "How fared your little parley with the Governor, Captain?"

Blackbeard's lips curved into a slow, enigmatic smile, a predator satisfied. "I believe, Israel," he said, his voice laced with the satisfaction of a wolf who has just dined, "it went exceedingly well."

Tick Tock; Tick Tock

"Will he betray us? The Crown will have his head for this!" Israel combs through his salt-swept hair with his hand.

"My gut tells me if you rogues keep your powder dry and his palms remain greased, his silence will be bought." Teach's words were more than a spoken thought; they were instructions.

Israel erupts in a raw, gut-wrenching bark of laughter that echoes off the salt-crusted timbers.

"Glorious! Absolutely glorious!" he gasped, wiping a phantom tear from his eye.

He strides back towards the town, the rhythm of his boots a defiant beat against the planks.

"And I think," Teach continues, his voice laced with a sudden, sharp edge, "I've even found a place to lay my head."

"A house?" The incredulity drips from Israel's voice, thick and viscous. "You, in possession of a dwelling?"

Blackbeard stops, the scent of brine and tar clinging to him like a second skin. He turns, his gaze sharp enough to flay the very air. "If the King himself deigns to pardon a scoundrel like me, then surely a man of my newfound respectability deserves a roof over his head, eh?" His laughter, a rumble like distant thunder, rolled through the air once more.

"Captain, I swear, the image of you... a homeowner... it's a jape that tickles my very soul," Israel admits, his own amusement still bubbling.

Blackbeard surveys the chaotic, bustling dock; the cacophony of shouts and creaking ropes is a symphony to his ears. He turns back to Israel, a predatory gleam in his eyes. "Two days. We give this port two days, and then we vanish back into the mist."

"Two days? Why such haste?"

"Because, my friend," Blackbeard's voice drops to a low, dangerous growl, "once you taste the wind in your sails again, you don't dare let it die."

Six grueling months have bled into the unforgiving sea. The Queen Anne's Revenge, a predator honed by hunger, slices through the churning waves, her sails taut against the bruised sky. Off the blighted coastline, the skeletal remains of a merchant vessel, a once proud ship now reduced to a writhing pyre, gasps its last, sinking into the greedy embrace of the ocean's depths. The scent of acrid smoke stings the air, a morbid perfume mingling with the salt spray. Supply ships, once a steady, comforting stream, have dwindled to a mere trickle, each meager arrival a desperate gamble. England, that distant, sputtering kingdom, has finally sniffed out the rat in her larder. The scent of Blackbeard's audacity has reached their nostrils, and the royal purse strings have tightened, the flow of sustenance choked. Whispers of their frantic search for new arteries of commerce, their desperate quest for new veins to bleed, slither on the wind.

Blackbeard stalks the scarred deck of his formidable vessel. The groan of timber, the snap of rigging, the rhythmic thud of his heavy boots, each sound a testament to their relentless pursuit. He watches, his gaze hard as flint, as the last ember of the doomed vessel winks out, swallowed by the indigo abyss. On deck, his crew, a pack of lean wolves, scrambled with a desperate urgency, their rough hands tearing at the meager spoils, separating the pittance of cargo and supplies. The air crackled with their hushed, anxious movements.

A shadow detaches itself from the periphery. Israel Hands, his face a roadmap of past battles and present fears, approaches, his voice a low rasp against the wind's howl.

"Captain?"

Blackbeard pivots, his massive frame a palpable force. The storm in his eyes mirrors the tempest outside.

"Yes, Hands?" His voice, a deep rumble, carried a chilling authority.

"What is our move, Captain? The ships... they are ghosts now. The bounty we once feasted upon... it thins." The unspoken question hangs heavy... "Are we to starve?"

Blackbeard's lips, a cruel slash across his weathered face, curl into something that might be a smile, or perhaps a snarl. "The word has indeed spread like a plague, eh? They fear us now. Good. Fear is a far more potent currency than any gold." He pauses, letting the weight of his presence settle. "Prepare to make a course for Charles Towne. We'll bleed them dry, sell what we can, and refill our coffers. And perhaps," his eyes gleamed with a predatory fire, "along the way, a stray lamb might wander into our path. A prize, ripe for the taking."

Here There Be Pirates

The air within Governor Spotswood's Manor hung thick and heavy, a suffocating tapestry woven from polished mahogany, aged leather, and the cloying sweetness of expensive wine. At the head of a table that stretched like a bloodstain across the opulent dining hall, Spotswood presided. Around him, Spotswood arranged his guests, a collection of the colony's gilded elite. Land barons whose fortunes were etched into the very soil and officers of the Crown whose polished brass gleamed with entitlement formed a predatory congregation around him. Lieutenant Maynard, a man whose gaze held the flinty edge of the sea, found himself nestled amongst them, a wolf amongst sheep.

Silent, specter-like servants glided through the gloom, their hands steady as they poured wine that shimmered like liquid rubies. Spotswood's own glass filled, and the crimson tide rose to the brim. He watched, his eyes, sharp as a hawk's, sweeping across the faces of his assembly before finally settling on the raw, hungry ambition reflected in their depths.

"My esteemed companions," Spotswood's voice, a low rumble that cut through the hushed reverence, began. "It fills me with no small satisfaction to see your esteemed presence gracing my table this evening. I have convened this gathering for a purpose of utmost urgency." He paused, the silence amplifying the unspoken weight of his words. "I have been in relentless communication with England, forging a desperate strategy to excise the rot of piracy before it festers and consumes our very shores."

Maynard's posture shifted, a subtle, almost imperceptible stiffening that belied the casualness of his surroundings. He leaned into his chair, his gaze now solely trained on the Governor.

"As you are all acutely aware," Spotswood continued, his voice darkening like an approaching storm, "whispers and outright declarations have painted a terrifying portrait of a marauder known only as 'Blackbeard. 'This phantom of the waves has been a scourge upon the Carolina coast, his avarice a gaping chasm, tearing at the very lifeblood of our commerce. He pilfers our cargo, then peddles his stolen spoils with impunity to every port and cove lining our coastline."

Maynard, his jaw tight, turned his head, the movement deliberate, to meet Spotswood's steely regard.

"Yes, Your Excellency," Maynard's voice, clear and resonant, sliced through the syrupy pronouncements. "But this has been treated as an isolated malignancy. Our most recent dispatches show the veritable plague, the true beast, lives in the treacherous waters of the Caribbean."

A flicker of something cold and sharp ignited in Spotswood's eyes, a chilling intelligence that belied the veneer of hospitality. He held Maynard's gaze, an unspoken challenge passing between them.

Spotswood raised his wineglass, the ruby liquid swirling in a hypnotic dance. The clinking of the glass against his teeth was a tiny, sharp sound in the oppressive stillness.

"I confess, Lieutenant," he said, his tone deceptively smooth, laced with a subtle venom, "my concern does not extend to the distant skirmishes and petty plundering of the Caribbean." He inhaled deeply, drawing the rich scent of wine into his lungs, then deliberately placed the glass upon the polished wood, the soft thud echoing like a drumbeat of finality.

"My sole obsession," Spotswood's voice lowered, becoming a dangerous whisper, "is this singular threat. And I fear, sir, that you, and perhaps many here, are gravely underestimating the festering nature of our predicament with him. England, already tightening the noose of taxation and starving us of vital supplies, grows impatient. The time for appeasement has long since passed. The time to strike is now. And it begins here."

The governor's chair scrapes violently against the polished floor, a raw, jarring sound that slices through the hushed conversation. He doesn't just stand; he erupts, his form casting a long, predatory shadow as he turns his back on the stunned faces of his guests. The air crackled with unspoken accusation. English politeness, a fragile veneer, shatters and crumbles to dust. The era of pleasantries is dead.

"Lieutenant!" The Governor's voice is a guttural growl, a command that echoes with the coiled fury of a viper.

Maynard, a man whose gaze has seen too much and yet yearns for more, rises from his seat. He walks, not merely paces, towards Spotswood, who stands like a statue carved from granite in the adjoining chamber, an island of unsettling calm.

"Yes, Your Honor?" Maynard's voice, a low rumble, betrayed a hint of something complex–anticipation, perhaps, or a flicker of unease.

Spotswood's hand, surprisingly warm yet firm, settles onto Maynard's shoulder, a touch that is both reassuring and possessive. Together, they move, not just into the parlor, but into a shared space heavy with unspoken pacts. The scent of beeswax and old leather hangs in the air, mingling with the fainter, metallic tang of something unseen.

"I don't want you to mistake me, Lieutenant," Spotswood's voice is a silken whisper, yet it carries the weight of iron. "What you spoke of tonight… I don't just agree. I feel it in my bones. Your mind for war, Maynard, it's a blade honed to perfection. A masterpiece." He leans in, the shadows deepening around his eyes, making them glint with almost feral intelligence.

"In a mere handful of days," Spotswood continues, his breath a warm current against Maynard's ear, "I will summon you. We will forge a plan, you and I. A plan to extinguish this… vermin. To grind him into the very dirt from which he crawled. Understand?"

A slow, knowing smile, a half-formed thing that hints at both pleasure and a chilling resolve, blossoms on Maynard's lips. It's a smile that promises darkness.

"Yes, sir," he replied, the words laced with a newfound, dangerous harmony.

The sun bleeds into the horizon along the South Carolina coast, its last, desperate rays painting the sky in hues of bruised purple and fiery orange. The dying light, like a weary sigh, trickles over the proud, stoic buildings of Charles Towne, their silhouettes stark against the darkening expanse of the harbor.

Blackbeard, a colossus of sinew and shadow, grips the salt-crusted rail of The Queen Anne's Revenge with a ferocity that threatens to splinter the ancient wood. His knuckles are bone white. In the distance, the tormented cries of burning ships, now ghostly wrecks, are swallowed by the hungry depths of the sea. He snatches his spyglass, its brass cool and heavy in his grip, and turns his gaze towards the inferno on land. Through the lens, he sees a tableau of terror: terrified townsfolk, their screams lost to the roaring inferno, fleeing the flames that devour their homes, their lives, their very souls. His own breath, rough and ragged, seemed to catch the acrid scent of smoke and despair.

Bay of Blood

Blackbeard's guttural roar ripped through the salty air, a primal sound of savage delight as the chaos he'd orchestrated unfolded before him. His eyes, like chips of obsidian, blazed with wicked glee. All his doing. Who dared whisper that the thrill had departed?

"Do you hear that, Israel?" Blackbeard's voice, a rumbling bass laced with the grit of a thousand battles, boomed. "That ye wouldn't find some fire again? Hah!"

Israel pointed a calloused finger toward Charles Towne Harbor. "Captain! A wasp trying to slip from its nest! The Crowley, she is."

Blackbeard snatched his spyglass, the polished brass cool and familiar in his calloused hand. He swept it across the scene, the tremor of anticipation a tangible force within him. He lowered the glass, his gaze locking onto Israel, a predatory glint in his eyes.

"Ours," Blackbeard declared, his voice hardening like tempered steel. "Whatever she is, she's ours. Tell them, Israel! Load the cannons on every deck! We're not letting that bird fly!"

He spun back towards the fore of the Queen Anne's Revenge, the wooden planks groaning under his weight. His voice, amplified by the wind and his own formidable presence, cut through the growing din. "Israel! Two shots! One to singe her sails, another to sting her hull! I'll be damned if she leaves this harbor!"

"Aye, Captain!" Israel's voice cracked like a whip. "You heard the man! Move, ye curs! Move!"

The deck of the Queen Anne's Revenge erupted into a flurry of controlled pandemonium. The air thrummed with the frantic energy of men who knew their grim purpose. Blackbeard stood at the stern, a colossus against the churning sea, his gaze fixed on the Crowley, a tiny, desperate speck against the vast canvas of the harbor.

Then, the earth-shattering BOOM of the cannons tore through the air, a visceral concussion that vibrated through bone and marrow. The deck beneath their feet bucked and recoiled, a savage beast lashing out.

On board the Crowley, a maelstrom of terror erupted. Figures scrambled like panicked ants, their cries swallowed by the deafening roar of the approaching storm. Officers, their faces grim masks of desperation, barked orders, their voices thin threads against the tide of fear.

Suddenly, a whistling shriek split the air, growing in intensity until it was a hungry predator's cry. A cannonball, a harbinger of destruction, screamed past, mere inches from a woman's outstretched hand. Her scream was a ragged shard of sound as the projectile continued its deadly trajectory, carving a path of devastation across the bay, narrowly missing the mainsail.

"By the beard of Neptune, did ye see that, Elias?" a terrified sailor yelled, his eyes wide with a horror that mirrored the faces of the cowering passengers he desperately tried to shield.

The helmsman, his knuckles white on the wheel, grunted his affirmation, his gaze fixed on the approaching doom.

The sailor, his voice raw with urgency, turned back to the terrified throng. "Get below! Now! To the hold, ye miserable souls!"

The Queen Anne's Revenge, a leviathan of wood and iron, bore down on The Crowley, her massive hull impacting with a bone-jarring crunch. The two ships lurched to a grinding halt, locked in a deadly embrace. Grappling hooks, like monstrous claws, arced through the air, biting deep into The Crowley's timbers, drawing them closer, closer, until the two vessels were no longer separate entities but extensions of each other.

Then, the boarding began. Pirates, a tide of snarling, bloodthirsty men, swarmed over the rails, cutlasses gleaming like ravenous predators 'teeth, pistols held ready to spit fire. Blackbeard, a figure of terrifying purpose, moved towards a nearby rope, his movements surprisingly fluid. With a single, decisive slash of his cutlass, he severed it. Then, with a theatrical flourish, he drew a flintlock from his baldric. He raised it to his face, the muzzle mere inches away. With a deafening crack, he fired. The ball hissed past his ear, igniting two primer cords woven into his already formidable beard. A fiery halo, a testament to his savage power, erupted around his demonic grin.

Man on a Mission

The monstrous shadow of Blackbeard erupted onto the Crowley's deck, a cyclone of grime and menace, landing with a guttural thud that vibrated through the ship's very bones. The stench of brine and something acrid, like stale blood, clung to him.

A wave of primal terror washed over the crew. They recoiled, a tableau of wide eyes and frozen limbs, pressed against the stern railing like cornered rats. The salty spray seemed to mock their fear.

Blackbeard's voice, a rasp of gravel and menace, shattered the stunned silence. "Bring forth every soul aboard this vessel! I want to feast my eyes on all who dare to breathe my air!"

His cutthroats, a pack of snarling wolves, descended into the bowels of the ship with brutal haste, their heavy boots pounding on the stairs like the drumming of doom.

From below, a cacophony of choked sobs and desperate whimpers rose. Women, their faces pale as death, huddled behind their men; their terror a palpable thing that chilled the air. One by one, someone dragged them, trembling, onto the main deck, and they blinked in the harsh light like terrified prey.

Blackbeard surveyed the trembling assembly. His men, their grimy hands reaching out, herded the passengers forward. They were a stark contrast to the pirates–finely dressed, their silk and velvet now stained with the grime of fear. Their silence was a heavy, suffocating blanket, broken only by the ragged gasps of dread.

Among them, a shadow within the shadows, stood Slipshot. Tall, his muscles bunched like coiled steel, he clutched a crumpled ship's manifest, snatched amidst the pandemonium. Blackbeard's predatory gaze locked onto it. "Slipshot! The manifest, you cur!"

Slipshot advanced, his heavy gait deliberately slow as he approached Blackbeard, the logbook held out like a sacrifice. In his passage, his eyes, sharp as shattered glass, met those of Samuel Wragg. Wragg, a portly man drowning in a deep blue coat adorned with gaudy gold trim, the very embodiment of Carolina's counsel, returned the look with a flicker of pure loathing.

They exchanged the manifest, a silent treaty of plunder. Blackbeard's voice boomed, a chilling approval. "Good work, my friends."

He opened the book, his scarred fingers tracing the lines. Then he froze. A name leaped out, a beacon in the dark ink. Samuel Wragg.

Blackbeard's head snapped up, his burning gaze sweeping over the cowering passengers, finally settling on Wragg. "Samuel Wragg!"

Wragg's head swiveled, his eyes wide with a terror that no amount of counsel could now quell. Blackbeard stalked towards him, his presence a suffocating weight. "Imagine my surprise, and my... pleasure, to find a man of your clear consequence gracing my humble vessel." A predatory gleam flashed in Blackbeard's eyes, a silent promise of torment. He then turned, his shadow stretching long across the deck.

"Now, listen closely," Blackbeard's voice dropped, a low, menacing growl that vibrated in every man's chest. "I shall ask you this only once. Do not betray each other with your cowardice. Where is this ship bound?"

A suffocating silence descended; the passengers frozen in a tableau of abject fear. The only sound was the frantic beating of their own hearts.

"We will spill your blood like cheap wine if you do not answer," Blackbeard's voice escalated, a venomous hiss that promised a gruesome end. "Do you understand me?"

Suddenly, a strained voice, thick with fear but laced with a desperate defiance, broke the silence. It was Wragg. "They are bound for London. Most carry provisions."

Blackbeard's lips curled into a sardonic smirk, his teeth a flash of white in his black beard. He regarded Wragg, a flicker of something akin to respect, or perhaps just amusement, in his gaze. "Ah, the richest among you speaks first. I had a feeling I could rely on such... pragmatism."

A chilling smile spread across Blackbeard's face, a macabre spectacle framed by his legendary beard. "Excellent. Now, escort these pampered pigeons back to their gilded cages." Blackbeard also ordered his crew to secure the prisoners in the darkest reaches of the cargo hold.

The pirates, their rough hands now imbued with a new purpose, herded the terrified passengers, their screams echoing in the confined spaces as they were driven back into the ship's suffocating depths. The crew of the Crowley, stripped of their ship and the darkness swallowed their dignity, leaving

Blackbeard alone on the deck, the scent of fear still hanging heavy in the salty air.

The dawn broke, a sickly yellow bleeding across the horizon. Inside the cramped, reeking belly of the ship, Blackbeard slumped over his desk, the rough wood biting into his forearms. Beside him, a half-empty bottle of rum, its cheap liquor a biting companion, glinted dully. He choked down a raw swig, the fire of it a meager warmth against the chill that had settled deep in his bones. Then, with a groan that seemed to echo the ship's weary timbers, he hauled himself to his feet.

The air in the crew's quarters was thick with the stench of sickness–a cloying mix of sweat, unwashed bodies, and the metallic tang of fever. As he stalked past the swaying hammocks, the spectral forms of his men writhed in their tormented sleep. Coughs, ragged and wet, scraped at the silence. Moans, low and guttural, vibrated through the very planks beneath his boots. These were not the sounds of brave warriors, but the whimpering of the damned, and Blackbeard's gut tightened with a familiar, corrosive rage.

He cornered the bosun, a hulking brute whose usual bluster was deflated like a pricked bladder. "What plague has us in its grip, Bosun?" Blackbeard's voice, usually a thunderclap, was a low growl, coiled with impatience.

The bosun shifted, his eyes darting away. "We've bled our stores dry, Captain. No more medicines. No more bandages. Naught but empty jars and withered herbs."

Blackbeard's gaze, sharp and unyielding, pinned the man. "A list, then. Draw me a list."

The bosun stammered, "A list, Captain? But where will we procure such things? The colony... they are not our friends."

A guttural bark of aggravation tore from Blackbeard's chest. "A list! I said, a list! Do you doubt my command?" The fury was a physical force, radiating from him, making the very air shimmer. He turned, the sounds of suffering a mocking chorus in his wake, and ascended the creaking stairs to the main deck, the salt-laced wind a sharp caress against his face.

On the heaving deck, Israel Hands stood by the railing, his gaze lost in the bay's expanse. The only sounds were the mournful song of the wind whistling through the rigging and the creak, creak, creak of strained ropes, a symphony of impending doom.

"Israel." Blackbeard's voice, now honed and chillingly calm, sliced through the quiet.

Israel turned, his eyes meeting Blackbeard's, a flicker of apprehension in their depths. "A quiet morning, Captain."

"Quiet for now," Blackbeard conceded, his tone deceptively smooth. He leaned against the railing, the weathered wood rough beneath his hand. "It seems our brave crew is succumbing to ailments we can no longer mend. Bring me that manifest again, Hands. We'll need a volunteer, a willing sacrifice, to fetch us what we require."

Israel produced the tattered parchment, its edges frayed by sea salt and time. Blackbeard's eyes, like chips of obsidian, scanned the list of passengers, a predatory gleam kindling within them. A slow, cruel smile stretched across his lips, revealing a gleam of yellowed teeth. "Ah, yes. We are depleted. And a volunteer is sorely needed. Someone to venture ashore and… negotiate."

From the shadows of the deck, Samuel Wragg, a man whose arrogance was as broad as his chest, stepped forward, his voice ringing with self-importance. "Since I seem to be the most… notable individual on this vessel, Captain, I shall undertake this mission."

Blackbeard's smile didn't falter, but a sharp edge entered his voice. "Nonsense, Wragg. Your talents are better suited to remaining aboard. You'll serve me better by keeping your seat. I have already appointed a man for this delicate task. A man named Marks."

From the depths of the ship, a figure emerged. Jonathan Marks, a wisp of a man, his hair like dried seagrass, his frame alarmingly thin, rose slowly. His eyes, downcast, clung to the deck as if it were the only solid thing in a world of shifting sands.

"You must be Marks," Blackbeard stated, his voice a silken threat.

Marks gave a barely perceptible nod, his head remaining bowed, a silent confession of his insignificance.

A longboat was being lowered, its descent into the choppy water a harbinger of desperation. Four of Blackbeard's most hardened men occupied its cramped confines, and between them, a rabbit in a den of wolves, sat Marks.

Blackbeard's voice boomed across the water, a final, chilling pronouncement. "You have two days, Marks. Two days to bend the Governor to your will and return with the medicines that will keep my men from the abyss. Fail, and you shall join them in their suffering."

Marks, his face a mask of terror, gave another jerky nod. The longboat, pushed by desperate oars, churned towards the harbor, a fragile vessel carrying an impossible burden.

And so it was, in the very harbor of Charles Towne, that Blackbeard's audacious presence became an unbearable affront to Governor Spotswood. Some whisper that he was merely bold, creating a spectacle of defiance. But a tempest of fury, a man reduced to a sea robber when his soul yearned for the boundless freedom of the open ocean, consumed him. His desperation, a beast unleashed, demanded tribute, and it would have it, by God, it would have it.

Blockade at Charleston

Three hellish days bled into the abyss, each agonizing tick of the chronometer stripping the crew's resolve to brittle threads. A creeping sickness gnawed at their insides, a festering despair mirroring the foul air that clung to the ship like a shroud. Blackbeard loomed at the salt-caked windows of his cabin, his gaze a predator's fixed on the unsuspecting arteries of Charles Towne harbor. Then, the air shattered. A frantic, desperate pounding, a frantic tattoo of knuckles against wood, clawed at the silence –

"CAPTAIN! CAPTAIN! For the love of all that's holy, come swiftly! The prisoners… they've gone mad!"

The cabin door, a bulwark against the brewing chaos, was ripped open with the ferocity of a storm surge. The bosun, a heaving mass of brine-soaked muscle, stood gasping, his face a mask of raw terror.

"They're in a frenzy, Captain! A damned mob! They think you're going to butcher them, they truly do, after these three days of… of this!"

A guttural chuckle, a sound like grinding gravestones, rumbled from Blackbeard's chest. "Let them howl. Let them shriek their fear into the void. Their lungs will burn out before they find peace."

From the shadows behind the Bosun, Israel materialized, his eyes glinting with chilling amusement. "Aye, Captain. They're a writhing knot of vermin, clawing over each other, convinced we're picking them off one by one."

Blackbeard's massive hand gestured with a contemptuous flick of his wrist. "Go. Whisper comfort into their hollow skulls. Tell them all is as it should be. Freedom... freedom is a promise that they will keep, soon enough.

He strode from his cabin, a colossus of dread, his boots echoing on the planks as he ascended to the main deck. The bosun scrambled ahead, Israel a silent, predatory shadow at his heels. Blackbeard advanced to the stern, the wind whipping his dark beard, a tempest in human form. Israel drew near, his voice a low growl.

"Captain, give the word. What is our command?"

Blackbeard's head swiveled, his eyes, like chips of obsidian, locking onto the helmsman and then Israel. "Turn these beasts. Face them directly at those docks. I want the fine folk of this town to taste the same curdled fear that festers in our bellies below."

A choked gasp escaped the helmsman. "Captain?"

"We are drawing a noose around this town," Blackbeard declared, his voice a thunderclap. "The Governor, that esteemed lord, cares for his flock. He will not suffer them to be torn asunder, nor his precious town to be reduced to rubble. He will yield. He must yield."

The great ships, with a groaning lament of timber and canvas, began their ponderous pivot towards the shore. A ripple of primal terror went through the huddled townsfolk as the monstrous hulls loomed, their escape routes vanishing like smoke. Panic, a tangible entity, seized them, and they scattered like frightened mice. Then, slicing through the mounting pandemonium, a cry from the crow's nest, sharp and urgent –

"Ahoy! A longboat is approaching off the starboard bow, Captain!"

Blackbeard's voice boomed, a challenge hurled into the wind. "Is it ours?"

He snatched his spyglass, his weathered hands steady as he swept the horizon. "Who is it, Captain?" Israel pressed, his gaze locked on his commander.

Blackbeard lowered the spyglass, a flicker of disbelief, then something akin to awe, contorting his rugged features. He turned to Israel, his voice rough with an emotion rarely seen. "I'll be damned. It's our men. Marks is with them."

He thrust the spyglass into Israel's hand. "See for yourself."

Israel peered through the lens, his breath catching. "I... I can't believe it."

"Nor I," Blackbeard rumbled, a rare smile cracking his grim visage. "The tide... it has turned for us, my friend. It has turned indeed."

And so, with a strategic brilliance that would echo through the ages, Blackbeard, the scourge of the seas, released the terrified townsfolk held captive in his ship's hold. Not a single soul bore the mark of his fury that day. It was a gamble, audacious and daring, and it had paid him handsomely.

Governor Spotswood, a man etched with the burdens of leadership, sat hunched over a vast document, his quill poised. A sharp, perfunctory rap sounded at his door. Spotswood's head snapped up, his eyes, accustomed to the shadows of intrigue, narrowing.

"Come."

The door swung inward, revealing Lieutenant Maynard, his face grim, his tricorn hat clutched in his hand like a fallen omen.

A Formidable Plan

The heavy parchment crackled like dry leaves under Spotswood's decisive hand as he set it down. The silence in the chamber seemed to thicken, charged with unspoken anticipation.

"You summoned me, sir." Maynard's voice was a low rumble, laced with an edge of... something. Not quite fear, not quite a challenge. It was the coiled tension of a predator.

Spotswood's gaze, sharp as a honed blade, locked onto Maynard's. "Indeed. And the hour has arrived." The words hung in the air, heavy with portent, like the scent of distant thunder.

Maynard tilted his head, a flicker of something unreadable in his eyes–amusement? Trepidation? "I confess, sir, your meaning eludes me." The rasp in his voice was a subtle whisper of gravel.

"It is time to drag this scoundrel to the abyss of justice," Spotswood's voice deepened, a guttural growl that vibrated in the soles of Maynard's boots.

"Have you not heard the latest exploits of the blockade at Charles Towne?"

"Naturally, sir." Maynard's response was a clipped breath, like struck flint.

Spotswood rose, his movement a predatory glide from behind his desk, the rich mahogany groaning faintly under his weight. His shadow stretched, consuming the room. "It appears we are adrift in a tempest of governmental disarray. My council gnaws at my authority."

"No one has breathed a word of such dissent, sir." Maynard's assertion was a low, almost mocking murmur, his eyes darting, searching the shadows.

Spotswood's finger, impossibly long and accusing, rose to his lips. "Apprehending this man… it will be the very balm my reputation craves. A beacon in this miasma of doubt."

Maynard took a step forward, the worn leather of his boots sighing on the floorboards. The air between them crackled, thick with the unspoken. "But sir, we haven't even a whisper of this man's whereabouts."

Spotswood's finger traced an invisible line in the air, a phantom threat. "True. Yet, I possess a knowledge of his intended trajectory. A clandestine whisper, you might say, carried on the wind."

With a deliberate swing, Spotswood crossed to a heavy oak door and threw it open. The sound was a violent rending of the silence. Within, a scene unfolded that struck Maynard like a physical blow. A man, his face a mask of gluttony, was devouring food with an almost desperate fervor. Beside him, a woman sat, her presence a smoldering ember in the dim light. Guards, their armor glinting like a hungry maw, stood sentinel. The air within the room was thick with the cloying sweetness of cheap perfume and the greasy aroma of unconsumed sustenance.

Maynard's breath hitched. "And who are these… unfortunate souls?"

Spotswood's voice was a silken threat, each word dripping with contempt. "The fellow to your left. He once peddled his wares in Bath town. A shop now reduced to dust and ruin, thanks to the shadow of Blackbeard's arrival. And the woman… she is but one of Blackbeard's countless playthings. A trinket he discards when the mood strikes."

"Really?" The word hung in the air, a chipped shard of disbelief.

Spotswood's bootfalls echoed, a percussive pronouncement as the heavy oak door slammed shut, sealing them in.

"What is it you command, sir?" Spotswood's voice, a low rumble like distant thunder, preceded him. He moved with a predator's grace towards the vast expanse of glass, the city a shimmering, indifferent tapestry far below.

"Two sloops. Fifty men. Yours to command." The words dropped like stones into a silent pool.

Maynard's breath hitched, his pupils dilating in the sudden, stark reality. "Sir, you cannot mean... an invasion of North Carolina?"

Spotswood spun, his gaze sharp enough to draw blood. "Not invasion. Not even soil. There's an inlet. Ocracoke. That's where he breeds." The air crackled with unspoken menace.

Maynard's boots scraped across the polished floor, a frantic urgency in his stride. "When do you propose this... undertaking?" His voice, usually steady, now held a tremor. "It demands planning, time..."

"Arrangements are complete." Spotswood cut him off, his voice a whip crack. "This entire campaign must remain veiled in shadow. The council... they would choke on its audacity." He closed the distance, the scent of expensive leather and something darker, something primal, clinging to him. "But succeed, Maynard, and the how will become irrelevant. The result will be all that matters."

Maynard's gaze, raw and unflinching, met Spotswood's. "You are the instrument. And the hour... the hour is NOW!" A challenge, a demand. "Can I rely on you?"

A guttural assent, a nod that spoke volumes of a man forged in the crucible of desperation and ambition. "You can, sir. You can rely on me."

A flicker of something akin to satisfaction, a tight, almost cruel smile, touched Spotswood's lips. A hand, surprisingly heavy, landed on Maynard's shoulder, a gesture of grim approval. "Good. That is precisely what I needed to hear."

Winter is Coming

Spotswood continued his deliberate stride towards his mahogany desk. Each step resonated with unspoken authority. "And Lieutenant," his voice, a low rumble like distant thunder, vibrated in the air, "if you manage to pull this off, a promotion of considerable weight awaits you. Beyond anything you've yet imagined."

Maynard, his jaw tight with a mix of anticipation and a healthy dose of fear, bowed his head, the gleam of his polished boots catching the faint lamplight. "Thank you, sir. It shall be done." The promise hung heavy, a gilded chain of obligation and opportunity.

A week later, the Hampton docks seethed with a chaotic symphony of urgency. The salty tang of the sea mingled with the acrid bite of gunpowder, a potent cocktail that set the nerves alight. Men, their faces etched with sweat and determination, heaved crates of powder kegs and bundles of shot, the rhythmic clang of metal on wood a relentless drumbeat. The air thrummed with the frantic energy of departure. Two leviathans of the sea, The Jane and

The Cornwall, bristled with preparations, their masts reaching like skeletal fingers towards a bruised sky. Maynard, his gaze sharp as a hawk's, patrolled the waterfront, a conductor orchestrating this feverish ballet.

He moved alongside the Jane, the groaning timbers of the gangplank a testament to the weight being hoisted. "Keep them coming!" he barked, his voice cutting through the din, a whip cracking against complacency. "We'll need every ounce. Every damned ounce."

Suddenly, a wiry sailor, his face smudged with grime, broke from the throng, his voice laced with desperation. "Lieutenant, sir! We're running out of space for the provisions! What are we to do?"

Maynard's lips curved into a slow, enigmatic smile, a flash of white against his tanned skin. He met the sailor's worried gaze, his eyes holding a depth of unspoken knowledge. "Fear not, my good man," he purred, his voice softening but losing none of its edge. "We're not sailing into the abyss. If hunger gnaws, we'll simply be close enough to shore to acquire what we need." The words hung in the air, heavy with implication, a hint of danger masked by a veneer of nonchalance. The sailor's shoulders sagged with relief, but a flicker of unease remained, a nascent understanding of the audacious game

Maynard was playing. "Better, now?" Maynard asked, a ghost of amusement dancing in his eyes.

The Queen Anne's Revenge lay like a slumbering beast in the shadowed embrace of Ocracoke Inlet, its menacing silhouette stark against the bruised Carolina sky. The salt-laced wind whipped at the tattered sails, carrying the raucous symphony of drunken revelry from the deck. Amidst the cacophony, Blackbeard strode the blood-stained planks of the stern, his gaze fixed on the turbulent expanse of the ocean. He moved with the predatory grace of a shark, a coiled spring of lethal intent.

He found Israel, a grim sentinel, etched against the horizon; his silhouette a testament to a life spent wrestling with the sea's indifferent gaze. The air vibrated with the raw power of the elements, a prelude to something far more potent than the fleeting warmth of the day.

"A sight to stir a man's soul, wouldn't you agree?" Blackbeard's voice, a gravelly rumble that scraped against the senses, sliced through the wind's howl.

Israel's eyes, deep pools reflecting the restless ocean, remained fixed on the distant line where sky met water. "It is," he conceded, his voice a low growl, a perfect counterpoint to the captain's burgeoning intensity.

"Few days bleed such vibrant hues into the canvas of our existence," Blackbeard mused, his massive hands, calloused from years of grappling with rope and blade, finding the cold, unyielding railing. The wood groaned beneath his touch, a silent testament to the sheer force of the man.

"Indeed."

Israel finally turned, his gaze, sharp as a honed cutlass, meeting Blackbeard's. The sea spray clinging to his weathered face glinted like captured starlight. "Finding solace in the sun, Captain?"

A half-smile, a predatory baring of teeth, split Blackbeard's face. "Every sunset, Israel, is a victory etched in crimson and gold. The breath that fills your lungs, a testament to a world still within our grasp." His eyes, like smoldering coals, promised a ferocity that belied the serene beauty of the moment.

"Aye."

"Savor this night, my friend," Blackbeard commanded, the words laced with an undertow of unspoken purpose. "Tomorrow, the ocean itself will tremble."

Miles away, where the frigid teeth of the Atlantic gnawed at the horizon, the Jane sliced through the churning, icy water. The wind shrieked like a banshee, hurling sheets of spray that stung the skin and tasted of salt and desperation. Maynard, a figure etched in grim resolve, approached the helmsman, his face a mask of calculated determination. Beside him, Jonathan Shaw, a young man sculpted from raw muscle and nascent ambition, moved with the quiet intensity of a predator in training. The ship's timbers groaned under the relentless assault of the waves, a testament to the unforgiving nature of their journey.

"We are close now," Maynard rasped, his voice a low growl against the gale. "Ocracoke by tomorrow's twilight, if the sea shows us even a flicker of mercy."

Maynard spun, the sudden movement a violent contrast to the controlled chaos of the storm, and collided with Shaw. "Is there a particular reason you stalk my wake, Mr. Shaw?" he challenged, his eyes narrowing, a spark of irritation igniting within them.

Shaw, unfazed by the spray and the captain's sharp tone, stepped back, his posture radiating a raw eagerness. "To learn from the master, Sir. To absorb every lesson the ocean can teach."

Maynard brushed past him, his stride purposeful, his voice dripping with a cool, dangerous skepticism. "That, Mr. Shaw, is a matter of perspective." He paused, a sudden, predatory glint in his eye, and turned. "You wish to learn, truly learn? Then cling to me for the next day. I will show you how to shatter an enemy's defenses, how to orchestrate a strike so devastating it will carve your names into the very bedrock of maritime lore." He continued his path, the weight of his words hanging heavy in the air. "Is that the knowledge you hunger for?"

Shaw fixed his gaze on Maynard's retreating figure, his chest heaving with renewed fervor. He surged forward, his voice a fierce cry against the storm's fury.

"Yes, sir!"

Months of relentless plunder, of carving a bloody swathe through every vessel that dared cross his path, had brought Blackbeard back to Ocracoke. Not for respite, but for the potent brew of anticipation that simmered in his veins. He returned to let his crew taste the fleeting sweetness of land, to sate their primal hunger for distraction, for on the morrow, the hunt would begin anew, a hunt that would echo through the annals of infamy.

Caught in a Trap

Israel's Adam's apple bobs as he drains the last bitter swallow from the bottle, the glass a cold weight as he slams it down on the scarred tabletop. The sound echoed in the sudden, charged silence.

"Tell me again," his voice is a low growl, laced with a dangerous edge, "why you dispatched the crew for the fleeting comfort of strangers 'flesh, while I'm stranded in this stew of yours, sharing my air with you?"

Blackbeard's laugh explodes, a guttural rumble that shakes the very timbers of the ship. It's a sound like grinding rocks, raw and untamed.

"Ah, Israel, my flinty friend!" Blackbeard's eyes, dark and glinting, locked onto Israel's. "Because, you see, your company is a rare and precious thing in this cesspool of cutthroats! Of all the stinking souls aboard this floating purgatory, only you, and perhaps one other, can wrench a laugh from my chest!"

A sardonic twist plays on Israel's lips. "A grim testament to your companions, if I'm the sole purveyor of humor."

A wave of shared laughter that spills into the night, a primal, unburdened release.

The first tendrils of dawn, tinged with the bruised purple of approaching day, bled across the horizon as Lieutenant Maynard's ship, the Jane, a phantom in the mist, glided with unnatural stealth into Ocracoke inlet. The notorious silhouette of the Queen Anne's Revenge, a dark leviathan, looms on the opposite shore.

A handful of pirates, sprawled in an unsettling stillness on the deck, are lost to the deep slumber of the debauched. Blackbeard, a hulking shadow against the nascent light, emerges from his cabin, his gaze sweeping the tranquil, deceptive expanse.

On The Jane, the disciplined urgency of the Royal Navy crackles through the air. Officers, their movements sharp and silent as striking serpents, orchestrate the covert ballet of preparation. They flowed across the deck, a tide of steel and purpose, descending towards the grim maw of the cannon ports.

Maynard, his jaw set, approaches the steersman, his voice a low, cutting command. "Take her in slow. Hug the left of those shoals. I want our arrival to be a scream, not a whisper. Let them slumber until the very last breath."

He lifts his spyglass, the polished glass a beacon in his grip, and brings it to his eye.

"Aye, sir!" the steersman replies, his voice a taut thread.

Maynard lowers the spyglass, his eyes burning, then rubs them with the back of his hand, a fleeting gesture of weariness. "Let us hope the gods of war favour our deception." The Jane, a predator disguised as prey, coils around the treacherous shoals, drawing ever closer to the unsuspecting heart of Blackbeard's empire.

Maynard's bloodthirst burns hot; his men, a coiled viper, poised to strike. The air crackles, thick with the unspoken promise of violence.

On the shimmering, molten edge of the world, Blackbeard stands a monolith. His weathered hand, calloused by a thousand storms and battles, shields eyes that have seen the abyss. A shadow falls, an omen etched against the blinding sun–the silhouette of a rival vessel, a predator breaching the horizon. He advances, a titan striding into the fray. "Hellfire!" The words tore from his throat, a guttural promise of reckoning. Blackbeard ignites the fuse of a nearby cannon.

Aboard the Jane, a frantic ballet of duty played out. The salt spray stings, the ropes groan, the wood creaks a weary song of the sea. Then, a violent interruption. A searing CRACK, a splintering roar that rips through the air, followed by a brutal, bone-jarring impact that slams into the Jane's flank. Wood shatters like bone, a gaping wound blooming on her side. Two souls, ripped from their anchors, are flung into the churning sea. Maynard drops low, the deck a shuddering beast beneath him. "Damn!" The word is a raw, ragged thing.

The steersman, his face a mask of grim terror, wrenched his gaze from the chaos to meet Maynard's. "He's seen us, sir!"

Maynard's voice is a whip crack, laced with a dangerous, gnawing frustration. "You think so?"

Panic flares, a wildfire across the deck. Officers, their faces pale as bleached bone, scrambled. "What should we do, sir?"

Maynard's gaze locks onto the treacherous teeth of the shoals, a desperate gamble painted against the shoreline. "Turn us towards those shoals!" he roars, the words carrying the weight of their impending doom. "It's our only salvation from another hellish volley!"

A chorus of fear rises. "But the sandbars, sir! We'll be dashed to pieces!"

His eyes, hard as obsidian, pierce through their terror. "It's the only path. We gamble with the sea, or we drown in her fury."

A rending CRACK, a splintering scream of timber, then the mainmast ERUPTS in a maelstrom of wood and rope! Men screamed and bled, buried beneath the shrapnel rain, as they were thrown like rag dolls.

Maynard, his face a mask of fury and desperation, roared, "Damn you all! HARD TO PORT!"

The helmsman, knuckles white, wrestles the wheel, the ship groaning in protest. "By the Devil's teeth, Lieutenant, one more blast like that and our mast is splinters in the sea!"

The Jane, a wounded beast, begins its agonizing turn toward the treacherous shoals. Behind them, the Queen Anne's Revenge, a vengeful shadow, closes the distance, its cannons hungry.

Maynard, rising amidst the chaos, surveys the devastation. A grim smile played on his lips. "If we're to sink, they'll have company in Davy Jones' Locker!"

Blackbeard prowls the main deck, his spyglass a glinting eye. Israel, his shadow, hovers nearby.

"Who the hell is that?" Blackbeard's voice is a gravelly thunder.

Israel snatches the spyglass. "No colors yet. A phantom, Captain. I know not."

Blackbeard's fist slams against the railing, the wood groaning under the impact. "Caught with my breeches down, am I? By some bilge rat with no colors?" His eyes, sharp as the Stygian darkness, dart to the deck where his remaining crew are arming themselves, a desperate, primal instinct.

"What's your play, Captain? Half the men are bleeding out!" Israel's voice strains with urgency.

Blackbeard's roar cuts him off. "I know our damned predicament! Do you think I'm blind?" He turns, a predatory gleam in his eyes. "Raise the mainsail!"

A ripple of disbelief. "Engage them? Now?"

"Damn right I will!"

"But the sandbars! The shoals! We'll run aground!"

"And if we run aground," Blackbeard sneers, a chilling amusement in his tone, "then they will run aground. And we'll be even. A fitting end for those who dare ambush me!"

Israel raises the spyglass again, his breath catching. "They're flying a Union Jack!"

"Unbelievable!" Blackbeard grins, a savage, unsettling sight. He began to load his pistols, the rhythmic click echoing the pounding of his heart. "We still out-gun them. And I'll fill their cursed hull with enough holes to drown a kraken! I'll send that ship to the bottom, colors and all!"

The Queen Anne's Revenge surges forward, a predator on the prowl. The two ships, no longer separated by fear but by a desperate, furious defiance, sailed in a lethal diagonal. The distance shrinks; the air crackles with anticipation.

Blackbeard, a titan armed to the teeth, ascends the stairs to the stern. He turns his spyglass once more to his eye, a hunter seeking his quarry.

"Captain!" the steersman shouts, his voice filled with panic. "The wheel! She's fighting me! We're going to run aground!"

Blackbeard ignores him, his gaze fixed. "Keep your course! I will know the face of the bastard who dared this insult!"

On the Jane, a palpable unease grips Maynard's men. Wounded men lie sprawled on the deck, their groans a mournful chorus. Maynard, his jaw set, descends from the stern, his presence a beacon of grim resolve.

Then, another CRACK, followed by a deafening BOOM that shook the very timbers of the ship! A side rail splinters into a thousand deadly shards as another cannonball tears into the Jane.

Maynard's voice is a raw, guttural cry, bellows, "HOLD FAST!"

"We're running aground, Captain!" The desperate cry ripped through the salty air, a raw shard of panic.

The Jane, a beast of the seas moments before, let out a tortured groan. A violent shudder wracked her timbers, timbers that had weathered a thousand storms, then–an abrupt, soul-jarring CRUNCH that echoed deep into the hull. The ship slammed to a halt, a sudden, violent stillness that betrayed the catastrophe.

Every soul aboard was a plaything of brutal physics. Laughter, curses, and the sharp crack of bone–the deck swallowed them all as men tumbled like drunken marionettes and their boots skittered across the slick, salt-crusted wood. The Jane, once a proud hunter, now lay exposed, her flank bared to the world, a wounded whale waiting for the kill.

A low, guttural chuckle rumbled from Blackbeard. It wasn't the sound of mirth, but of a predator savoring the scent of weakness. His eyes, like chips of obsidian, gleamed with a dark delight as he surveyed the Jane's ignominious plight. He spun, his massive frame eclipsing the frantic activity behind him, and barked an order to the steersman, his voice a lash of authority.

"Two degrees starboard, you dog! And hold yer powder until I give the word. The reckoning ain't yet begun."

A hive of frenzied activity erupted among his crew. The air grew thick with the metallic tang of gunpowder and the acrid scent of oiled cannons. The crew readied fuses, like coiled serpents, their brittle ends poised. The crew brutally shoved the monstrous cannons, hungry mouths of iron, to the portholes.

As if to mock the Jane's first insult, the other vessel, now also a victim of the treacherous sandbar, lurched and groaned, its own agonizing plight mirroring the first.

Then, Blackbeard's voice, a thunderclap that split the very air, roared, "FIRE!"

"FIRE!" "FIRE, ye devils!" "Unleash hell upon them! Give 'em all ye've got!"

The world dissolved into a deafening symphony of destruction. The air vibrated, not with the fury of the sea, but with the concussive roar of a hundred cannons spewing their fiery breath. The decks of Blackbeard's ship bucked and strained, the very souls of its timbers screaming under the immense force of the broadside.

Last Stand

The Jane heaved, a gut-wrenching shudder that vibrated through her very timbers. Cannonballs, like monstrous iron beasts, snarled across her main deck, tearing through canvas sails with savage finality and slamming into the proud masts, splintering them into jagged teeth. The air exploded with the screams of men, sharp and raw, as the indiscriminate fury of the bombardment found its mark.

Then, an unnerving hush. The acrid bite of gunpowder smoke stung the lungs, clinging to the air like a shroud. As it thinned, a brutal tableau emerged. The two vessels, angled like vengeful arrowheads, were impaled on the sandbar, a mere stone's throw – perhaps two hundred yards – from each other. The silence stretched, taut and expectant, broken only by the ragged gasps of wounded men and the creak of tortured wood.

A sudden, cool breeze, a phantom sigh, swept across the carnage, lifting the clinging smoke and revealing the stark reality of their predicament.

On the bow of his vessel, a silhouette of pure menace, Blackbeard clung to a frayed rope, his knuckles white. In his other hand, a flintlock pistol glinted, a promise of more violence. He roared, his voice a gravelly challenge ripped from the very depths of the storm, "Who the hell are you?"

The question hung, unanswered, swallowed by the vast, indifferent sea.

"Answer me, damn you!" the demand came again, laced with the impatience of a predator denied its prey.

From the ravaged deck of the Jane, a nervous tremor of voices, a rustling of fear, finally broke the silence.

Maynard, his face a mask of grim defiance, stood rigid along the ship's rails, his gaze locked onto Blackbeard's predatory form. "As you can see from our colors," he bellowed back, his voice strained but clear, "we are no pirates!"

Blackbeard's eyes, dark pits reflecting the glint of the sun, bored into Maynard. "Indeed!" The single word dripped with derision. He descended from the rails; Israel, a hulking shadow, immediately at his side. A handful of his hardened crew, their faces etched with brutal curiosity, followed close behind.

"These men are cracked!" Israel growled, his voice a guttural rumble.

"Not cracked, Israel," Blackbeard corrected, a cruel smile playing on his lips. "Stupid is a more appropriate descriptor." He gestured with his pistol towards the battered Jane. "Does he expect us to board?"

A flicker of disbelief crossed Israel's hardened features. "This ship and these men are Royal Navy!"

Blackbeard's laughter, a harsh, barking sound, echoed across the water.

"Who else," Blackbeard spat, his eyes narrowing with a chilling intensity, "would be this desperate to capture me?" The unspoken threat, the raw audacity, hung heavy in the salt-laced air, a prelude to an even fiercer storm.

The tattered sails of The Queen Anne's Revenge, like starved lungs, greedily inhaled the biting kiss of a rising gale. Blackbeard, a titan etched in shadow and menace, lifts his gaze to the towering masts. His voice, a gravelly roar ripped from the very depths of hell, cracks through the din:

"Fire another shot! I want to see this whelp's guts spilled across the waves! Cripple the bastard!"

On the Jane, Maynard and the dwindling, desperate phantoms of his crew brace themselves. A thunderous CRACK rips through the air, a prelude to oblivion. "Brace yourselves!" A molten orb of destruction screams past Maynard, a harbinger of death. It slams into his deck, not with a simple impact, but with a visceral, rending violence. The air erupts in a symphony of splintering wood and screaming metal, shards of oak flying like shrapnel, each one a tiny, deadly projectile. The very bones of The Jane groan and tear.

The colossal blast, a monstrous exhalation from the Queen Anne's Revenge, severs the ship's tortured connection to the sandbar, yanking it free with a violent shudder. Amidst the chaos, a sailor, his face a mask of raw, unadulterated terror, scrambled closer to Maynard.

"Take the remaining men down below and arm yourselves with everything we've got!"

"Aye, sir!" The response was choked, a guttural assent from men facing their own mortality.

The very soul of the Queen Anne's Revenge seemed to shudder with the force of that cannon shot, a seismic jolt that finally liberated the Jane from its sandy prison.

Blackbeard, his eyes burning with a primal, savage gleam, orchestrates the frenzy amongst his remaining rabid pack.

"Scour every bilge! Find every empty rum bottle! Fill 'em with powder, with shot, with chunks of lead that'll tear flesh! Jam a fuse down the heart of each one. Save your true ammunition for the bloodletting when we board! When we're close enough to taste their fear, light the devils! Hurl them onto their decks! Let them dance, the fools!"

The Legend Lives On

The acrid sting of gunpowder and salt still hung thick in the air, a choking shroud that clawed at his throat. As it grudgingly yielded, his eyes, burning and raw, locked onto the deck of The Jane. A handful of shapes, dark and menacing, resolved themselves into men. Maynard. Not a whisper of him.

But the beast, The Revenge, was a snarling predator, its iron maw closing on The Jane. The hull groaned, a guttural beast of the sea, grinding against its prey.

"Grappling hooks, you scurvy dogs! Ready yourselves to rend flesh!" The order ripped through the air, a raw, primal bark. Every pirate, a coiled viper on deck, assumed their deadly crouch, muscles tensed, mind alight with savage intent.

"NOW!"

The world erupted into a symphony of tearing metal and snapping wood. Hooks, like the talons of fallen gods, clawed at the rails of The Jane, teeth biting deep. The ropes, taut and straining, became the

sinews of their conquest, yanking the two ships into
a brutal, agonizing embrace.

"Light the damned fuses, you devils! Let the heavens
weep fire!" The command was a thunderclap.
Grenades, crude thunderstones, flared to life in the
men's grimy hands, their fuses spitting angry
tongues of flame. Then, a deadly rain descended.

The impact was a concussive roar. Grenades
detonated with a sickening CRUMP, a symphony of
destruction. Splinters of wood, sharp as shrapnel,
rained down, a deadly confetti. A coil of rope, ignited
by the inferno, writhed like a serpent, and patches of
The Jane's deck became infernos, licking greedily at
the night.

Through the swirling inferno of smoke and flame,
Maynard stood, a grim silhouette against the infernal
glow, his remaining crew a spectral presence. "What
are we to do, sir?" a voice cracked, raw with fear.

Maynard's hand, steady despite the chaos, cocked
his pistol. Then, with a metallic rasp that promised
oblivion, his sword was drawn. "Wait for my signal,"
his voice was a low growl, laced with chilling resolve.
"Then we charge. Let the devil take the hindmost.
Kill them all."

"Aye, sir."

Blackbeard, his gaze a predatory gleam, surveyed the carnage. Then, a guttural roar, a challenge to the very firmament, tore from his chest. "Bring hell to the heavens and rain down fire!"

The pirates, a tide of pure savagery, screamed their war cries and surged onto the Jane's burning deck. Blackbeard, a figure of nightmarish grace, severed a rope and swung across the chasm, his heavy boots landing with a thunderous impact amidst the smoke and screams.

Maynard's men, a desperate surge, burst through the haze. All hell broke loose.

Blackbeard's eyes, burning with an unholy fury, scanned the inferno for his quarry. He found him.

A naval officer, a ghost in the smoke, lunged. Blackbeard's pistol barked, a single, deafening crack. A crimson bloom bloomed between the officer's eyes, and he toppled backward, a marionette with its strings cut.

At that precise, terrible instant, Maynard materialized from the swirling haze.

Blackbeard, with a primal snarl, hurled his pistol. He snatched another pistol from his baldric, cocking the hammer with brutal efficiency. He aimed. And FIRED.

"There you are, you son of a bitch!"

The ball tore a searing path, not a killing blow, but a brutal kiss that ripped through Maynard's neck. Maynard, astonishingly, did not falter. His own pistol roared, its shot a punishing embrace that found Blackbeard's shoulder. The massive pirate barely grunted, his rage a palpable force.

Blackbeard's sword, a glinting serpent of steel, lunged. Maynard met it, his own blade singing a defiant, desperate song. But Blackbeard's strike was a thunderclap, landing on Maynard's sword with such brutal force that the blade snapped, its fragments scattering like broken promises.

Maynard PANICKED.

"CHRIST ALMIGHTY!" He slammed to the deck, a desperate roll over the cooling corpse of a seaman. His eyes, wide with terror, scrabbled for a weapon. He found one, a bloodied cutlass.

Blackbeard advanced, a relentless tide of destruction. Another blow fell, a hammer blow of death. Maynard blocked, scrambling to rise, but Blackbeard struck again, a vicious slash that ripped through the front of Maynard's shirt, exposing the pale flesh beneath.

"You attack me like a coward? This is your reward!" Blackbeard's blade, dripping with a dark sheen, pointed, a chilling accusation, at Maynard's throat.

"Who the hell are you?" Blackbeard demanded.

"Robert Maynard. Lieutenant."

Blackbeard's laughter was a cruel, mocking sound that echoed through the charnel house of the deck. "You're not much of a military man, are you? Your name sounds… familiar. I killed a naval officer called Maynard in the Caribbean. Any relation?"

Blackbeard grinned, a predatory baring of teeth, as Maynard's eyes widened in dawning horror.

"At the end," Blackbeard spat, the words dripping with venomous triumph, "he begged for his life. BEGGED!"

Maynard's primal roar tears through the cacophony of battle, a visceral sound that shatters the air as he lunges, his cutlass a silver blur aimed at Blackbeard's hulking form. The dance of death begins, a brutal ballet of steel meeting steel. Each jarring impact sends violent vibrations up their arms, a percussive symphony of CLANG! CRACK!

Sparks, like furious fireflies, erupt from the grinding metal, briefly illuminating the desperation etched on their faces. The metallic tang of blood and sweat hangs heavy, mingling with the salty spray of the sea.

Blackbeard, a titan of fury, yields ground, his immense power momentarily faltering. Then, a phantom of the shadows, Shaw, erupts from the swirling chaos, a man possessed. His sword, a gleaming fang, drove deep into Blackbeard's gut, a sickening thud that echoed the gasp torn from Shaw's own throat. He drives the blade deeper, the rough texture of the hilt grating against his own spine, an agonizing testament to his ferocity. Blackbeard's roar is no longer of anger, but a primal bellow of pain and incandescent rage, a sound that promises an eternity of retribution.

Across the blood-slicked deck, Israel's eyes, sharp and haunted, locked onto his captain's plight. A guttural cry escapes his lips as he carves a path through the milling throng, each strike a desperate plea, a desperate bid to reach the stern. His breath comes in ragged gasps, the taste of brine and copper thick on his tongue.

"Captain!"

In that sliver of distraction, a fleeting moment of vulnerability, a nameless sailor emerges from the periphery, a shadow made real. A harpoon, sharp

and unforgiving, punches through Israel's chest with
a wet, tearing sound, stealing the air from his lungs.
He collapses onto the deck, his lifeblood blooming in
a dark crimson stain.

Blackbeard's head whips around, his eyes, blazing
like twin infernos, fall upon Israel's lifeless form. A
shattering shot rips through the air, biting into
Blackbeard's chest. Then another, a sickening impact
that makes him stagger. A third follows, each blow a
hammer blow against his tormented flesh. He snarls,
a beast cornered, and fumbles for a pistol. With a
ragged breath, he fired, the shot a thunderous retort,
striking Maynard in the leg. A searing agony flares,
but Maynard's gaze remains locked, burning with a
righteous fury.

"I will kill you where you stand, damn you!"
Blackbeard spits, the words laced with venom.

From the periphery, Shaw reappears, a whirlwind of
desperation. A glint of steel in his hand, he lunges,
plunging his knife into Blackbeard's throat with a
savage thrust. A choked gurgle, a violent expulsion of
crimson, and Blackbeard reacts with the raw power
of a wounded bear, his elbow connecting with
Shaw's head, sending him reeling.

Shaw crashes to the deck, the impact jarring, his
body landing atop a discarded sword. With a
desperate heave, he rolled off, his hand snatching the

weapon, sliding it across the groaning timbers towards Maynard.

"Lieutenant!"

Maynard, gritting his teeth against the searing pain, snatched the blade. Blackbeard, his face a mask of unadulterated hatred, bellows a challenge and brings his own sword down in a murderous arc. Maynard recoils, the wind whistling past his ears, his boots skidding on the blood-soaked deck. But he's a survivor. He recovers, his arms a blur, twisting the swords, their steel singing a death knell. With a final, guttural cry, he unleashes a fatal blow, a downward slash that severs Blackbeard's head from his neck.

The grotesque trophy separates; a sickening thud as it lands. Blackbeard's massive frame buckles, his knees giving way. He collapses onto the deck, a broken titan, his reign of terror definitively, irrevocably, DEAD.

The air on the deck of The Jane hung thick and cloying, a morbid perfume of salt, blood, and the iron tang of spilled life. Maynard, his boots crunching on a gruesome carpet of crimson-soaked wood, surveyed the carnage. Dead pirates, their faces contorted in final, desperate snarls, lay sprawled amongst the shattered forms of naval officers and common seamen. The very planks beneath their feet seemed to weep with the violence that had unfolded.

And there, amidst the carnage, lay Blackbeard–
Edward Teach, a titan felled, his monstrous head a
few agonizing feet from his sprawling corpse.

"You promised a lesson today, Lieutenant," Shaw's
voice, rough as barnacles scraped from a hull, cut
through the unsettling silence.

Maynard turned, his gaze hard as diamond, locking
onto Shaw. "Death. I know death, Shaw. Unmerciful.
Brutal. The kind that scars the soul." His voice, a low
growl, resonated with a chilling familiarity with the
abyss.

Two weary sailors, their faces etched with the
horrors they'd witnessed, shuffled towards them,
their footsteps echoing the hollowness in their eyes.
"Lieutenant," one stammered, his voice cracking,
"what... what are we to do with Blackbeard's body?"

Maynard's lips curled into a grim smile, a predator's
baring of teeth. "Take his head," he commanded, his
voice sharp as a cutlass, "and let it dangle from the
bowsprit, a grisly flag. His body? Give it to the sea.
Let the sharks feast on the King of Pirates."

The sailors exchanged a bewildered glance, their
confusion a stark contrast to the grim finality of
Maynard's words. "The bowsprit, sir? Why there?"

"So that every scurvy dog who sails these waters can
feast their eyes upon it," Maynard spat, his eyes

burning with righteous fury. This will be a stark, screaming testament.

With a nod, the sailors turned, their movements heavy with the weight of their grim task. The sickening thud of bone against wood, the guttural tearing of flesh–sounds that would haunt their dreams for years to come–soon followed.

"You truly believe that will silence them?" Shaw asked, his voice laced with a doubt as deep as the ocean.

Maynard's gaze drifted to the horizon, a glint of something unreadable in his eyes. "We shall see, Shaw. We shall see."

The Jane, a specter of victory, began to glide away from the hulking, derelict Queen Anne's Revenge. Then, a thunderous roar split the air. A cannonball screamed, tearing a ragged hole in the pirate ship's decaying hull. Another followed, then another, each impact a hammer blow on the coffin of a dying era. Slowly, with a mournful groan that seemed to echo the screams of the damned, the Queen Anne's Revenge surrendered to the embrace of the sea.

As the Jane melted into the shimmering expanse of the horizon, a legend was being forged in blood and brine. Blackbeard, in his ignominious end, had achieved the ultimate apotheosis. His name, once a whisper of terror, now blazed into myth, spreading like a conflagration through every port and tavern. To some, his demise brought a sigh of profound relief, a lifting of a suffocating dread. To others, it was a source of bitter sorrow, the extinguishing of a dark, captivating flame.

As the sun rose on that sliver of sand. On the beach, that small band of men listened intently. The bonfire is now mere embers. The tale had come to an end. Hornigold's voice, a gravelly rasp honed by rum and years of violence, cuts through the dawn. "Edward knew. He knew that in the tales that would be spun for generations, the whispers of black flags and daring raids would fade. They wouldn't remember the men who dared to defy empires. No, they would remember the one man who embodied pure, unadulterated savagery—the one who brought hell itself in his wake." Hornigold swipes his boot, extinguishing the remains of the orange glow from the fire.

"Captain Edward Teach. Blackbeard. The last pirate the world would ever know. And Maynard, the instrument of his downfall, had become a part of that legend."

www.ingramcontent.com/pod-product-compliance
Lightning Source LLC
Chambersburg PA
CBHW071925150726
47999CB00001B/110